"What holds the special magic of this te
and the juxtaposition of its narrative m
most vibrant, intimate, and passionate v
and pains. A beautiful mosaic work wh:
moved as if from a dream." —France TV, Culturebox

Author & Translator Biographies

MICHÈLE AUDIN is a mathematician and a professor at l'Institut de recherche mathématique avancée (IRMA) in Strasbourg, where she does research notably in the area of symplectic geometry. Audin is a member of the Oulipo, and is the author of many works of mathematics and the history of mathematics, She has also published a work of creative nonfiction on the disappearance of her father, *Une vie brève* (Gallimard, 2013)—Audin is the daughter of mathematician Maurice Audin, who died under torture in 1957 in Algeria, after having been arrested by parachutists of General Jacques Massu. On January 1, 2009, she refused to receive the Legion of Honor, on the grounds that the President of France, Nicolas Sarkozy, had refused to respond to a letter asking for information on her father, the possible whereabouts of his body, and recognition of the French government's role in his disappearance. For the Oulipo, Audin has contributed to a collection of short stories, *Georges Perec and the Oulipo: Winter Journeys* (Atlas Press, 2013), and edited and annotated an abecedary of Oulipo works, *OULIPO L'Abécédaire provisoirement définitif* (Larousse, 2014). *One Hundred Twenty-One Days* is her first novel and was published to universal acclaim in 2014 by the prestigious Gallimard publishing house in France.

CHRISTIANA HILLS is a literary translator who graduated from NYU's MA program in Literary Translation (French–English) and who received a French Voices Award from the Cultural Services of the French Embassy in the United States for her translation of *One Hundred Twenty-One Days*. Hills is currently a doctoral candidate in Translation Studies at Binghamton University in New York.

ONE HUNDRED TWENTY-ONE DAYS

—

Michèle Audin

TRANSLATED FROM THE FRENCH BY
CHRISTIANA HILLS

DEEP VELLUM PUBLISHING
DALLAS, TEXAS

Deep Vellum Publishing
3000 Commerce St., Dallas, Texas 75226
deepvellum.org · @deepvellum

Deep Vellum Publishing is a 501c3
nonprofit literary arts organization founded in 2013.

ISBN: 978-1-941920-32-9 (paperback) · 978-1-941920-33-6 (ebook)
LIBRARY OF CONGRESS CONTROL NUMBER: 2015960719

—

Cet ouvrage a bénéficié du soutien des Programmes d'aide à la publication de l'Institut Français.
This work, published as part of a program of aid for publication,
received support from the Institut Français.

French Voices Logo designed by Serge Bloch

This work, published as part of a program providing publication assistance,
received financial support from the French Ministry of Foreign Affairs,
the Cultural Services of the French Embassy in the United States and FACE
(French American Cultural Exchange).

—

Cover design & typesetting by Anna Zylicz · annazylicz.com

Text set in Bembo, a typeface modeled on typefaces cut by Francesco Griffo
for Aldo Manuzio's printing of *De Aetna* in 1495 in Venice.

Distributed by Consortium Book Sales & Distribution.

Printed in the United States of America on acid-free paper.

Table of Contents

———

KALLE: I like the way it moves towards the war.

ZIFFEL: You think I should arrange it in chapters after all?

KALLE: What for?

B. BRECHT,
Conversations in Exile

[…] (the form of a city
Changes more quickly, alas, than the human heart)

C. BAUDELAIRE,
"The Swan," *Parisian Scenes*

CHAPTER I

A Childhood

(1900s)

I start to write:

Once upon a time, in a remote region of a faraway land, there lived a little boy. And this little boy was full of an insatiable curiosity and he was always asking ever so many questions. The faraway land where he lived was in Africa, in a country that encompassed a big river called the Saloum River, and the little boy filled the land around this river with his questions.

He asked his father why the Blacks on the plantation were beaten with a stick, and his father spanked him with his leather belt. He asked his mother why she didn't read her Bible by herself, and his mother spanked him with her two white hands. He asked the village priest why he drank the communion wine during Catechism class, and the priest spanked him with his cane. He asked the schoolteacher why the same number, π, was used to measure all circles, both big ones and little ones, and the schoolteacher didn't spank him.

I must tell you, O Best Beloved, that some good fairies were watching over this little boy's cradle. If there were a few evil fairies as well, no one noticed. So there will be no discussion of evil fairies at this point in the tale.

★

A fairy tale is one way to recount history. The Saloum River, its village, its plantation, its pirogues, and its flame trees form the setting for this tale. The little boy's parents, his little brother, the fairies, the priest, the schoolteacher, a dog, and a few of the villagers are its characters. The little boy who lived in this exotic setting at the center of this little world was named Christian. The good fairies, along with the schoolteacher who didn't spank anyone who asked questions, were responsible for the fact that he really loved going to school, where he was taught to read books, to write fast and well, to count fast and high, and to ask questions. As for his parents, they thought that the time he spent at school was much too long. Because you see, although his mother liked that he could read the Gospels aloud to her, his parents wondered why he needed to learn any more. One day, while spanking him with his leather belt, the boy's father said: "Well, you're not going to become a writer, in any case!" Because, O Best Beloved, at this time on the banks of the Saloum River, there were public writers who would write letters for people and read them the letters they received. And, you see, the little boy's father was working hard to make the Negroes sweat on the peanut plantation, and he thought that the writer, who spent all his days sitting in the shade of a kapok tree right in the middle of the village, was a lazy man.

One fine morning, at the beginning of summer, the schoolteacher came to the plantation and explained to the little boy's parents that not only could their son read and write fast and well, but that he also knew how to do sums using very big numbers, and that it would be good to send him to secondary school, in the big city, so that he might learn all that can be done with all those big numbers and all that reading and writing. But you see, O Best Beloved, at this time and in the land around the Saloum River, no boy had ever gone to secondary school. His parents listened politely and said they would think about it. Yet as soon as the schoolteacher left, they fought, his mother kicked, his father punched, then they both started spanking the little boy without wasting any more time. They even called the priest over for help. The boy's little brother was also spanked for good measure. A little later, when that was over, the little boy came across a yellow dog that belonged to one of his friends, and said to him:

"My father has spanked me, and my mother has spanked me, and the priest has spanked me. And still I want to go to secondary school in the big city to learn how to do calculations with even bigger numbers and learn more about the number π."

And the little yellow dog licked the little boy's face affectionately as the little boy scratched him behind the ears.

Naturally, a few days later, the schoolteacher came back to the plantation, then the mayor, then the schoolteacher once again. Each time, they negotiated, but with no success. Until the day when the schoolteacher came back saying that he had found a scholarship, and the parents agreed to let the little boy leave. They all spanked him once more for luck. Then he went away, a little swollen. It was a fine morning, at the time of the equinox. The little boy rode down the Saloum River with his little suitcase. On the pirogue, the chickens had been pushed out of the way to clear a comfortable place for him. It was the beginning of his new life.

After the pirogue, the little boy took a steamboat that eventually brought him to the big city. The world around him had expanded. At school, he went straight into seventh grade. He was a very good student, both a quick learner and a hard worker. He was eager to learn so that he could find answers to the questions that stirred his insatiable curiosity. He even got caught up in German, because at that time, O Best Beloved, they learned German at secondary schools in the big cities of faraway lands. It was useful to learn German. The little boy learned some poems by heart that were written by a German poet named Heine. He really liked the story of the *Two Grenadiers,* from which he would recite a verse to himself:

Der eine sprach: "Wie weh wird mir,"

which translates as, "The one said: 'How I suffer,'" and which could indeed be useful to know. In this way, he found answers to some of the questions he had about war. He also took Latin and Greek. He really liked poetry and would often recite another poem to himself, which said:

You'll be a Man, my son!

You see, he thought that this poem was speaking to him, because it said "you," just like this story is meant for you, Best Beloved.

At school, no one spanked him. The teachers loved him and pampered him, especially the German teacher. So he was happy. Yet you must know that even though he really liked German, his favorite class was mathematics. That was also where he excelled the most. In mathematics, you were allowed to ask ever so many questions.

And even to come up with new ones as soon as you found the answers to the old ones. And he loved numbers, logical reasoning, and even the most complicated figures in geometry.

And then he was fifteen. So his teachers came up with the idea of having him prepare for the exam to get into the École Polytechnique, which was, they said, the greatest school in Paris and the world. This couldn't be done at the secondary school in the big city in the faraway land. The teachers wanted him to go to Paris, which is the largest and most beautiful city in France, as you know.

So the teachers wrote to the schoolteacher at the edge of the Saloum River; the schoolteacher went to see the boy's parents on the peanut plantation; the boy, who had taken the steamboat and the pirogue to spend the summer with his father, his mother, his brother, and his yellow dog, was spanked from all sides; his little brother was also spanked for good measure; the yellow dog licked his face affectionately; his teachers found a scholarship; the father put his belt back on; and in the end, everyone left in single file towards the banks of the Saloum. There, the boy, who was a little swollen, climbed into the pirogue, and the chickens were pushed out of the way to clear a comfortable place for him.

You can't go all the way to Paris just by taking a pirogue down the Saloum River. After the pirogue and the steamboat, the boy still had to get on an ocean liner, then a train. But this is perhaps where an evil fairy appeared and Christian fell gravely ill. It was an illness with a fever and delirium, and so he had to be taken to the big hospital in the big city. He stayed there for several weeks, while the boats he didn't get on left for France. It looked like he was going to die, but as you know, children don't die in fairy tales. While he was sick, there were times when he had nightmares filled with demons, like the ones the priest in the village on the banks of the Saloum used to describe in Catechism class. And there were also more peaceful times when he thought about geometry problems and also a little about his nurse. In the hospitals in big cities in faraway lands, the nurses were actually nuns. The one who was taking care of the boy wore a cornet on her head, a wooden cross, and all those other things nuns wear. You had to call her "sister," but that didn't prevent Christian from seeing she was just a girl, and he liked her very much. At that time, boys and girls didn't go to the same secondary schools. And so this boy had never met any girls. White girls, of course—there were black girls on the plantation, on the banks of the Saloum, but at that time, Blacks didn't count.

★

And here's where the setting expands even more, where other characters get involved in the story, which is going to become so complex that the fairy tale, with its good and evil fairies, will not be enough to tell it. The story will have to find other forms, other methods. But know this: little Christian's life is far from over—it will last over one hundred years. Around him, others will live and die, which we must also take into account. For the rest of the novel, when he will have become a man, Christian needs a last name—first names by themselves only work for children. So it's time to choose one for him, Mortsauf, maybe, or Mortfaus or Morfaust…

★

The story isn't over but the fairy tale ends here, at the moment when young Christian, fully recovered, climbed bravely up the gangway of the ocean liner while thinking about his yellow dog. And the ocean liner, which was called *Afrique*, carried him over the Atlantic Ocean and the Mediterranean Sea, past the Canary Islands, Morocco, and Spain, to the railroad at Marseille. Then it was the Gare de Lyon and the greatest city in the world, with its coachmen, its Champs-Élysées, its Eiffel Towers, its numbers, its polytechnical schools, its theorems, and all of its pretty girls who reminded him of the pretty nun who had taken care of him at the hospital.

CHAPTER II

Diary of Marguerite Janvier

(1916-1917)

February 2, 1916

At the hospital again today, my sad contribution to the war effort. A nurse… what else can we do, we women, while all of our valiant men are at the front? To give myself courage, when I wake up and cross Paris on foot in the frosty night towards the Val-de-Grâce hospital, I only need to think of their sacrifices. What suffering!

Today, a young man came to us, almost a child, who left the hospital three weeks ago. That had already been his second injury; we gave him a few days of convalescent leave, then he left again for the Chemin des Dames and was injured once more. This time it was shrapnel—they had to amputate his right leg when he was still in the ambulance. And here, we trepanned him. As stoic as I must appear, my heart tightens when I think about him. At least they won't send him back to the front this time. I pray that God grants courage to his poor mother, because she's going to find him in such a state! And with only one leg, how will he be able to go back to working on a farm?

February 10, 1916

The Germans are barbarians. There is no other word to describe these bombardments, these injuries, these mutilations! Barbaric! All this suffering in order to satisfy the monstrous pan-German ambition!

The most unbelievable thing is that these monsters call themselves Christians. They worship a god of terror and dedicate these sacrifices to him. Fortunately, we too have powerful weapons, thanks to which God will help us to conquer them and to defend both civilization and Christian values.

I spoke about this with a history student who was leaving our unit. He had been trepanned, his head injury had been treated, but he left with an empty shirt sleeve. He was crying as he told me about his best friend, who jumped out of a trench and was killed, at age nineteen, when he would have gone on to become the greatest poet of the century. When it comes to the Krauts, he concluded, you have to give them an eye for an eye.

The house is freezing. Mama is trying in vain to get the stove repaired.

February 29, 1916

Lots of snow these past few days.

This year has one more day than usual. For me, it's one more day of war. They've been bringing injured men from the front—the battle rages in Verdun.

Today one of the wounded men in the unit was telling everyone about the date, February 29. 1916 is a leap year, and according to him, there are magic numbers in it. He's a Jew, but also a former polytechnician who is very well raised and amiable. He has only been here for a few days and probably isn't going to stay for very long, because his injury is pretty minor: a shell blew up near him and his head collided with a large stone. The problem is, all of his comrades were killed, which is also terrible for him, the sole survivor.

I know this because the major told me, but the patient himself doesn't talk about it. It's true that the men here hardly speak about what they've gone through at the front. Usually, he remains peacefully in his corner, studying. He cries from time to time while writing mathematical formulas, but today he seemed rather excited and was looking at me in a strange way. Oh, that his god would give him the strength to bear his sadness!

Tuesday, March 7

Lots of snow fell again during the night. I had a really hard time getting to the hospital. How can one not picture the shroud that must be covering the battlefields? But can the snow's whiteness mask such horrors?

Wednesday, March 15

Father de La Martinière told me that I should pray for a Jew's soul, and so I now include Robert (that is, the polytechnician) in my evening prayers. He's going to leave the hospital soon, and so I'm spending as much time with him as I can. How wonderful it would be to win over this soul to the true religion!

"Mademoiselle Marguerite, give me a number please!" he shouts out as soon as he sees me enter the room. I say a random answer, but he claims I always give him the same one. "No, not 11, you already gave me that one yesterday," he tells me, so I say another number, 6. "Thank you," he responds and starts calculating again. "It's just that I'm solving equations, Mademoiselle Marguerite," he says.

This morning, I asked him if he believed in heaven, and, with his eyes shining their brightest, he looked at me and said:

Then hell was silent.

Three injured men in the unit died today, almost at the same time.

October 4, 1916

When I was leaving the hospital this evening to go home, Major de Brisson held me back and asked if I would agree to change units—he said they need me in facial surgery. The major was a friend of Papa's at boarding school, and he still comes to the house often, so I couldn't refuse. He wants me to start tomorrow.

Maybe, in this unit, I won't have any more time to think about Robert. That's my hope as I start writing in this notebook again today. It will be no more time than I spent telling Mama about it, no more than I spent telling the priest about it, because there was nothing to confess, it seemed, and I just couldn't write in here about what happened the day he left. Only the thought of Mama kept me from asking to be moved to a hospital at the front.

Sunday the 8th

I haven't been able to write since last Thursday. As I was leaving mass this morning, I decided to force myself to. But how can I put down on paper what I do, what we do in this unit? Opening up their skulls, trepanning under chloroform—you have to approach it like it's nothing. Nothing compared to changing the dressings, discovering the bruised flesh, the empty eye sockets, the... I can't even finish my sentence. Lord, give me strength. They've suffered terrible injuries at such a young age, and now they're disfigured for life. That's what I said to Mama and Thérèse. I know Thérèse tries to imagine what's under the bandages, but I know she can't. You have to see it to believe it.

The hardest thing in this unit is when I have to tell them they're free from harm. Not getting flustered when I say things like "You're safe," or "You made it through." Afterwards, they ask me what's under the bandages, what they look like, if they're very disfigured. I promised to show two men their faces tomorrow morning, I'll let them borrow the mirror from my handbag. There's a third one recovering who is disfigured, but blind—at least he won't have to see his "broken face." It's late, I have to stop writing and seek a little strength in prayer.

Hail Mary, full of grace.

October 16, 1916

I am the bearer of bad news. I force myself to smile. They look at themselves in the mirror and they cry. One tried not to cry and started gallantly singing:

> *Farewell to life, farewell to love,*
> *Farewell to all the girls,*

but he burst into tears. I know this song, it continues with:

> *'Cause we've all been sentenced to die,*
> *We're the ones being sacrificed.*

How can you accept not being able to recognize your own face? The worst thing is that most of them refuse the comfort of religion. They prefer to spend their time hiding away with bottles of alcohol. How those got here, I don't know.

October 18

And they continue to suffer. By the time they get here from the front, their jawbones have started to grow back together, but so poorly that many have difficulty eating. For some, it even hurts to speak.

October 23, 1916

Mama and Thérèse left last Friday to spend a few days at our house in Normandy; they brought enough material to knit blankets for our poor heroes who are starting to get cold again, especially in the mud. It's the start of the third winter of war.

As I'm alone at home, I worked on Saturday and Sunday (I even heard mass with the men), and I'm getting home later in the evenings.

Today, while bringing medicine to one of our patients, I heard the young man in the next bed over breathing strangely. This patient's face is so badly damaged that he can only breathe through his mouth. I quickly understood at that point that he could no longer breathe at all. The cause was a hemorrhage that was filling his throat with blood. I lifted up his head and drew out as much blood as I could with a syringe.

Then I ran to find Doctor Debalme, who arrived a few minutes later. He wasn't pleased that I hadn't called him first; he told me rather firmly that I was only a nurse and it wasn't up to me to decide if blood needs to be drawn out, since it's a medical procedure.

October 24, 1916

Major de Brisson called me in this morning and congratulated me on saving the life of the young man with the hemorrhage. He said, "Marguerite, you saved him and you did well. Doctor Debalme would have arrived too late."

The patient is an artillery lieutenant. He was really unlucky—it's rare for an artilleryman to be wounded in the face. The majority of those whom we treat here served in the infantry, they're the ones who charge out of the trenches and take the most hits.

Tuesday the 31st

This morning, I again had to show a truly disfigured young man his new face. He's the one who had the hemorrhage last week. He still has his left eye, his left check, and a bit—a tiny bit—of his left jaw, his forehead, and his chin. There's a big lock of hair on his right temple that is growing back red, like an extra scar in his brown hair. A single bullet managed to do all this damage. But it must be said that it was practically shot point blank.

He's the first of my patients who didn't cry at seeing his destroyed face. But he is very young, still a student.

I don't dare write anything about him because he is a polytechnician like Robert. There has already been another mathematician in the unit. That one left blind a week ago; he told me he was going to do a dissertation on geometry. I thought of Robert. I wonder what he's doing now; maybe he's still in the infernal trenches. I continue mentioning him in my evening prayers.

We have taken back Douaumont.

My cousin Jacques was killed in Verdun.

We have never done so many operations in the unit as we did today.

November 8, 1916

This morning, I was taking off the polytechnician's dressings so that he can undergo a bone graft (he already had a xenograft when he arrived; today they're trying an autograft, using a fragment from one of his tibias), when he recited the following to me:

You'll be a Man, my son!

He added that he really liked Kipling. I think I smiled, and then answered:

But I do not tremble in seeing my weakness.

He recognized it as one of Papa's verses and said he really liked the poetry of Albert Janvier. I felt myself blush and said that the poet Albert Janvier was my father. Then I told him about how Papa died, the railroad accident, but I couldn't talk for very long—they were taking him to the operating room and other unfortunate men were awaiting treatment.

I wonder if he has a fiancée. I think about all those girls whose lovers will return disfigured, and all those whose lovers will never return… I don't know which will need more courage.

The worst will perhaps be for those who won't know, because their men will have been declared missing.

November 14, 1916

Today, a surprise: Cousin Paul, dressed in full mourning attire, came to the unit. He had come to see a patient, and it was Lieutenant Mortsauf, my polytechnician! They spent the whole afternoon together, talking about mathematics. Paul had brought some books. I listened to their conversation while I was treating the others in the room—they were discussing things and writing formulas on sheets of paper that were then falling all around them onto the floor. When Paul left, I came over to remove the polytechnician's stitches from his last operation. As I picked up the papers, he said, "So, Mademoiselle Marguerite, I take it you know Professor de Saint-Bonnet?" When I replied that he's Mama's cousin, he commended me. I told him that one of Paul's sons had been killed in January and another last month, but he knew. He said that Paul was going to help him make use of his time at the hospital and that he was going to write a dissertation.

Friday, December 1st

As I move throughout the room, treating the other patients, I can see the polytechnician filling entire pages of his little yellow notebooks with calculations. Paul comes to see him two or three times a week. Sometimes he brings other mathematicians, and the patient always introduces me to them as "Mademoiselle Marguerite, the nurse who saved my life." He tells me he owes his "second birth" to me. He explains his work to them; sometimes he tears sheets from his notebook and they take the papers with them. I don't understand what they talk about, and besides, I don't have time to listen, but I know that when they're here, he smiles more. Even underneath the layers of gauze, I can discern a smile as soon as one is there. Today I heard them speaking in the stairwell as they were leaving.

Paul was crying and I could see his colleague had teary eyes. I know Paul was thinking about his two sons. Jacques, his oldest, was so brilliant, and he hadn't even had time to start working on anything. At least he died gloriously. Glory and honor are also (I don't dare write what they are above all) death and tears.

December 11, 1916

Last week, like he asked me, I brought home a few pages from the polytechnician's notebook to write out a clean copy in the evenings—that's why I haven't had time to write in this diary.

I told him I really like his handwriting, but I don't understand any of it and I hope I don't write something foolish or add in mistakes.

Maybe I spend a little too much time talking to him. I worry that the other patients in the room, behind the beige curtains, resent me. So I try to speak with some of them as well. I give words of comfort to those coming back from rehabilitation sessions, where heavier and heavier weights are attached to their lower jaws in order to help their muscles get used to opening their mouths, in spite of their deformed jawbones. Sometimes I write letters for those who don't know how to write very well. Last night, I even played charades with two of them. Although I had to force myself at the beginning, we were soon laughing together. But laughing also makes them suffer.

I've finally finished copying the one hundred twenty pages that Christian (Lieutenant Mortsauf asked me to call him by his first name) gave to me. Fortunately, his handwriting is very readable. When I told him once more I didn't understand any of it, he laughed and replied "Of course you don't understand any of it, it's not for girls, do you expect a girl to understand the transcendence of π?" But he seemed very satisfied. I could see him smiling under the bandages then, too.

The battle of Verdun is finally over. Major de Brisson says 300,000 men died there. But their sacrifice was not in vain because the victory was ours.

I stayed very late at the hospital yesterday evening. The doctors aren't finished with my polytechnician, so he's going to have to stay here for the holidays. In any case, his family is in Africa, and it would be out of the question for him to get leave to visit them. He told me about the village where he was born, where his parents run a peanut plantation. He described a big river, with the Negroes' pirogues, the pelicans, and beautiful trees called flame trees. He told me about his mother, Saint Theresa of Avila, Saint John of the Cross, and a little yellow dog, a kind of retriever, that he loved very much and that had died. If I were a man, I think I would like to travel and see such places. But a woman's place is the home.

He told me, very tenderly, about a nurse, a young nun who had cared for him in Africa. He also mentioned his injury and the evil fairy Carabosse.

December 21, 1916

I brought him a few books.

Friday, December 22

I stayed very late at Val-de-Grâce, but Major de Brisson drove me home. It was nighttime and very cold. I was so moved by what happened today that I couldn't speak in the automobile.

I spent the evening with my injured soldier; together we read the books I had brought him. He didn't really appreciate Dante, whom I like a lot. I opened the book to the page where the song of Ulysses begins. "It's very beautiful," he said, "but I prefer Shelley," and he quoted:

The soul's joy lies in doing.

I must confess that I thought of Robert again. But we mainly read Papa's poems:

Jesus, the wounded one, the sinner, the wanderer
Washes his ailing heart in the flow of Your blood.

That's when I felt a real bond between us. Then we talked a lot; he asked me how we had fared after Papa's death, I explained how he had made some shrewd investments, and how since Mama was wealthy, too, we were living quite comfortably. He seemed pleased with this, as well as when I said that Papa had bought a beautiful house in Normandy and that we also owned an apartment on Rue d'Artois, where Papa had worked and which Mama was renting out. It's really nice of him to be so interested in us.

I have leave for Christmas, so I'm going to spend the holidays with Mama and Thérèse.

Christmas

I got up early this morning and decided to take stock of my feelings in this diary.

I have to revisit what happened with Robert in March. He needed a lot of support, both morally and, I think, spiritually. I admit, I really enjoyed our conversations. But I didn't expect him to ask me to marry him. Naturally, I refused. He asked me why, like a child, and I answered that we were too different.

I haven't even told Mama about it. I know Papa would never have agreed for me to marry a Jew, Papa who, along with Cousin Paul and a few others, founded the League of the French Homeland during the affair with that man Dreyfus.

Wednesday the 27th

I returned to the hospital today. Lots of work, as if the Germans wanted to celebrate Christmas by killing as many of our men as possible. Yet there's talk of a truce here and there. I didn't have time to talk to him.

January 2, 1917

Today I had to try to comfort two wounded men who were crying because they were thinking about their fiancées. "I'm a monster," one was saying, "She won't want me anymore," the other was saying, "No one will want me," said the first, all of this in sobs.

I hope their fiancées will think of the sacrifice they have made for our country and will love them for their moral greatness. I asked to pray with them, but one told me that while he would be grateful if I could pray for him, he could never pray again. The other, who works in an automobile factory in civilian life, turned his back and pretended to sleep.

The weather is so misty and sad.

January 5, 1917

Lieutenant Mortsauf has finished writing his dissertation. Cousin Paul will come get it tomorrow. In the meantime, I wrote out the dedication in beautiful lettering, for which he thoughtfully put:

> "To the Polytechnicians Who Died on the
> Field of Honor in a Just War"

with all those pretty capital letters.

He told me he was very satisfied with what he had done, and I'm sure it's true, given how happy he seemed.

January 8, 1917

So much work. I couldn't even stop to eat at midday.

No time to write again this evening.

January 9, 1917

He's still working in his yellow notebooks. Paul told him he'll probably win a prize for his dissertation. He also told me Paul was his Saint Christopher. I didn't really understand what he meant by that.

When I congratulated him for the glorious prize he was going to receive, he answered:

> If you can meet with Triumph and Disaster
> And treat those two impostors just the same;
> (…) You'll be a Man, my son!

Thursday, February 1st

Today I begin a new notebook, the third for this diary I've been keeping in secret since Papa's death. I was so young then!

I haven't had very much time to write. I've often stayed late in the evening to talk to the men, who also need moral support. I've talked to Christian the most. We told each other what we like— I told him I like flowers. He told me he likes dogs. I really prefer cats, and I told him so. He told me that his dream, before the war, was to have a house with three dogs and six children, six boys. I told him I'd really like to have a little girl.

He's going on a few days' leave to defend his dissertation. I would've liked to go but I didn't dare say so; after all, it's not the place for a young lady, and I couldn't imagine asking permission to leave the hospital for that.

So much snow again this year.

Thursday, March 1st, 1917

At least we haven't had a February 29th this year. A year already, I remember the numbers: 29 and 479, which are prime numbers, Robert had shouted to everyone in the room, as if to announce some good news. "But why 479?" one of the patients had asked, while the others, with their bandaged heads, tried to escape the racket. "Because," Robert replied, "if there is a February 29th, it's because 1916 is divisible by 4, so divide it, divide it!" he had shouted.

Today, while I was changing his dressings, my patient took out a photo of himself from under his blanket. "That's how I was before. No one will want me now," he said—him, too. I told him as gently as I could that he must not say that.

I prayed for God to give me the strength to understand my feelings more clearly.

March 2

I looked at Jesus on the cross above my bed. He is wounded, too. I took His cross in my hands. I looked at His unfortunate face and He drank my tears.

March 3, 1917

I told Mama that Christian asked if I would agree to marry him.

I don't dare think back on the mean things Thérèse uttered. And yet, I will. She said he wants to marry me because we're rich and we have relatives in high places, and besides, I'm not even pretty. And she also said I agreed because I want to show everyone I'm capable of sacrifice, so that, along with my angelic airs, I would appear patriotic. Mama was angry and made Thérèse be quiet while saying I have beautiful blue eyes and "la beauté du diable" (the beauty of youth), and as for Thérèse, who thinks she's so pretty, we'll see how she looks at age thirty after having a few children, if someone still wants her in spite of her meanness.

Mama trusts my opinion.

On my table, a moonbeam lights up the white statue.

Our Lady of Lourdes, please help me.

March 5, 1917

I spoke to him. He asked the hospital for leave so that he can come see Mama and make his request. His father is much too far away for this to be done by the rules.

I will be Madame Christian Mortsauf.

April 2, 1917

We have set the date, June 23, a Saturday. It will be at Saint-Philippe-du-Roule, our parish, and Father de La Martinière will marry us. Then we will leave for our "honeymoon" at our house in Normandy.

Today, the cherry trees there must be in blossom.

His parents won't be able to come. Not only is it too far, but, with the Krauts' submarines ready to torpedo any innocent ships that pass, it would be too dangerous. Jean-Baptiste, his younger brother, will get leave to come. He and Cousin Paul will be Christian's groomsmen. Major de Brisson and Thérèse will be my bridesmaids. Grandfather will walk me down the aisle.

You will be there in the church, Mary, full of grace, and you will support me with your love.

I would have loved a simple ceremony, but Father de La Martinière and Major de Brisson insisted, because of the symbol it will be: Christian will represent all of his comrades lost in combat and will wear the full uniform of the École Polytechnique, with the medals for the Croix de Guerre and the Légion d'Honneur. He was fitted for a mask in black taffeta, which hides the scars and reproduces the shape of his nose. That way he can go without the bandages and wear the cocked hat—I hope the red lock of hair will show from underneath. Cousin Paul, although he is still in full mourning, will wear the green uniform of the French Academy. This means I had to go and be fitted for a dress that is far more complicated than what I would have wanted. I cried when I saw myself in the dressmaker's mirror. Is this really me? I feel more myself in my canvas blouse. At least the veil reminds me of my nurse's uniform.

Mama is busy doing up the apartment on Rue d'Artois, where we will live.

He is different, too. His family isn't from the same background as ours. But Cousin Paul says his career looks very promising, and his family is far away.

Besides, Papa would have been happy to know I'm marrying a young man with such a bright future, who is a good Catholic and a polytechnician.

CHAPTER III

One Polytechnician, Three Murders, Twenty-Two Articles

(1917–1939)

A POLYTECHNICIAN MURDERS HIS ENTIRE FAMILY

(Le Petit Parisien, June 25, 1917)

Yesterday in Le Chesnay (Seine-et-Oise), Roger Goldstein, former student of the École Polytechnique and lieutenant in the 6th Artillery Regiment, killed his father, his mother, his brother, and one of his aunts, who was a nurse at Hospital 209. The family was gathered around their Sunday lunch when the madman fired the mortal gunshots. Alerted by the racket, a female neighbor went to get the police, whom the murderer obeyed without any difficulties.

THE AMERICANS ARRIVE!

(L'Ouest-Éclair, June 30, 1917)

After General Pershing's arrival in Paris on the 13th, last Tuesday saw the first American soldiers disembark at the port of Saint-Nazaire.

THE MURDERER HAD HIS SENSE KNOCKED OUT OF HIM!

(Le Petit Parisien, July 2, 1917)

We have been informed that Robert Gorenstein (and not Roger Goldstein, as we printed in error), the polytechnician and officer on leave who was arrested last week for the murder of his uncle, his aunt, and his brother (three and not four crimes as was written in haste in a previous article) was a victim of an artillery shell last January. Almost all the men in his battery were killed, and he himself hit his head.

In a horrible development, according to information gathered from neighbors, the three Gorenstein children were orphans and had been raised by their aunt and her husband.

At the time, military doctors considered him recovered, and he was sent back to the front. He is presently undergoing psychiatric exams.

DEATH OF A FLYING ACE

(Le Soir, September 15, 1917)

The aviator Georges Guynemer died on Tuesday in Poelkapelle (Belgium). He achieved more than eighty victories in the "Storks" fighter squadron.

A PLAGUE VANQUISHED

(Le Petit Parisien, October 2, 1917)

Typhoid fever has disappeared from the French front.

COUP D'ÉTAT IN RUSSIA

(L'Humanité, November 9, 1917)

The Maximalists are the rulers of Petrograd. Kerensky has been deposed. The fallen government no longer has the support of the Soviets.

Lenin has won the Soviets' acclaim. The new government is calling for peace.

BOLSHEVIK NEGOTIATIONS

(Le Matin, December 15, 1917)

The Bolsheviks have started peace negotiations with the Krauts. If they reach an agreement, the liberated German troops will be free to come reinforce our attackers.

DERANGED POLYTECHNICIAN SHUT AWAY

(Le Petit Parisien, January 17, 1918)

The verdict in the Robert Gorenstein affair was announced yesterday. Readers may recall that he was arrested in June after murdering three members of his family. During the trial, the polytechnician, who had injured his head in battle at the Chemin des Dames, declared that he had wanted to eradicate the dead branches of his family. The psychiatrist deemed him irresponsible and as harmless as a little boy, now that he considered his task accomplished.

In view of this expertise, the court pronounced a sentence of life internment in a psychiatric ward.

★

PIERRE MEYER (interview, December 18, 2006). *Marguerite never spoke about Gorenstein to anyone, I believe. Until 1945, when her daughter Bernadette left home. She went to get her notebooks from the bottom of the big wardrobe and gave them to Bernadette, asking her to read and save them. The newspaper clippings about the triple murder and the trial were slipped into the notebooks. She had stopped writing when she got married. She gave them to her daughter and died not long afterwards.*

The article on typhoid was also among her papers. It appeared right around the time her sister died of typhus. She was eighteen. Marguerite named her first daughter, Thérèse, after her.

Bernadette was the fourth. Why she was the one Marguerite gave her diary to, I'm not sure I really ever knew.

★

THE G. CASE: A FIRST REPORT

BY J. MEYERBEER, PSYCHIATRIC DOCTOR, SAINT-MAURICE

(Gazette of the Association of Psychiatric Doctors of France,
Vol. 28, 1920)

One may recall the bloody criminal story that the daily newspapers had a field day with in 1917–18, probably after being tired of publishing news from the front passed through the sieve of military censure. A multiple family murder, a matricidal (or almost) polytechnician—none other than a journalist would have more reason to celebrate. The goal of this article is to present the patient and his current state, two years after he was hospitalized.

HISTORY

Let us briefly recall the facts. On June 24, 1917, Robert G., then 22 years of age, killed his uncle and aunt, Monsieur and Madame H., and one of his sisters, Cécile G., during a family meal. More specifically, as he himself confessed and as the investigation confirmed, he started by shooting his youngest sister, then his aunt, and only killed his uncle when the latter interposed. Monsieur and Madame G. died in an accident when their son Robert was only two years old. Madame H. was his mother's sister. She and her husband, who had no children, took on the responsibility of raising Nicole, Robert, and Cécile G., then aged four, two, and one. The three children did brilliantly in school; only Cécile, the youngest, was still living with her adoptive parents.

A student of the École Polytechnique, Robert G. had been

mobilized as a second lieutenant of artillery. The only one from his battery to survive after a violent German attack in February 1916, he was hospitalized for a head injury, then sent back to the front in April. During the events of June 1917, he was on a few days' leave.

At the court's request, he was the subject of a psychiatric appraisal performed by our esteemed colleague, Doctor Bergamotte. The latter shared with us his remarks on the report he submitted to the judicial authorities, for which we are grateful. Briefly:

- the subject was perfectly conscious during the crime,
- he acted for reasons of eugenics,
- he declared himself satisfied with having eradicated the deficient branches of the family.

From the doctor's interviews with the patient and the exams he performed on him, Doctor Bergamotte concluded that Robert G. would be harmless from that point forward.

The judge—acting very prudently where a combatant was concerned, one who, moreover, was wounded in the war—was lenient and decided to have him interned. He has been at the Saint-Maurice Hospital, in our unit, for three years.

We would like to highlight the fact that Robert G.'s eldest sister, Nicole, who is two years older than he, was not present at the fatal lunch. She is very attached to the patient. She was also a witness at the trial. Her love for her brother, in spite of the crime committed against the family, stupefied the jury and bore weight on the decision as well.

REMARKS ON THE HOSPITALIZATION

Robert G. is living in a locked room that has been furnished for a long-term stay.

He is a calm and amiable patient. For this reason, he is well-liked by the staff. He demands far less attention than the noisy, agitated patients who are brought in here wrapped up like dolls.

He seems to be very satisfied with his situation. Dressed in a hospital gown and a black velvet cap, he spends his days reading and writing.

He willingly goes along with our questions, enduring them with a look of indifference, which might be feigned.

He asked to be allowed to use books. He wrote a list of the ones he needed himself, and we asked his sister to bring him the desired volumes. With the exception of Goethe's *Faust*, they are all books on mathematics. A bookshelf and a table have been set up in his room so that he can write.

He has returned to studying mathematical science, to which he had had little time to devote after he left the École Polytechnique, on the very eve of the war. He asked permission to correspond with mathematicians from France and other countries (but not Germany), to which we agreed.

As he himself has made us note, he can work peacefully, without having to be preoccupied with teaching classes or engaging in other lucrative activities needed to earn a living.

We will add that he reads a passage from his copy of *Faust* every evening. This act of reading and the evocation of hell make him cry. Each time we ask for an explanation of these tears, he launches into a long series of reflections which are unclear (and repetitive), with recurring mentions of succubi, which are, according to G., demons with blue eyes.

He receives regular visits from his sister, sometimes accompanied by her husband.

A VISIT TO VAL-DE-GRÂCE
(L'Humanité, July 14, 1920)

Here, faces are remade. Just a glimpse at the two photos included in this article will allow you to judge the doctors' work completed on the broken faces of our soldiers.

THE SOLEMN HOMAGE OF THE GRATEFUL HOMELAND
(Le Petit Parisien, November 12, 1920)

The coffin of the "Unknown Soldier," placed on a cannon, pre-ceded by the chariot carrying Gambetta's heart, arrived at the Arc de Triomphe yesterday.

DID YOU SEE THE ECLIPSE?
(Le Petit Parisien, April 9, 1921)

The extreme clarity of the atmosphere allowed curious amateur astronomers to contemplate yesterday's solar eclipse in all its beauty. The classic method? Good old cheap smoked glass.

★

PIERRE MEYER (interview, December 18, 2006, cont.). *She felt a tremendous amount of compassion for her husband. His injury caused him to suffer for his entire life. He must have not been very easy to live with. Terrible temper. And that huge household she had to look after, six children! They were very close in age: the youngest, Ignace, was born in 1924. They named him after Mortaufs's brother, who was killed in 1918. Such an atrocious war…*

It was at that time, when Ignace was born, that they bought the house in Chatou. Marguerite had a personal fortune, and Mortaufs was earning a good amount of money, with all those courses he was teaching in various places.

★

ANNOUNCEMENTS
(Le Figaro, October 24, 1922)

The professor Christian Mortaufs
and Madame,
née Marguerite Janvier,
announce the birth
on October 18, 1922, of

BERNADETTE MARIE BAPTISTINE

The baptism will take place
on Tuesday at 10 o'clock in the morning
at the Church of Saint-Philippe-du-Roule

22, Rue d'Artois, Paris, 8th arr.

———

Claude Duvivier
lawyer at the Paris Bar,
and his wife Nicole,
née Gorenstein,
have the joy of announcing
the birth of their daughter

MIREILLE ANNE

on October 17, 1922
9, Rue de Médicis, Paris, 6th arr.

THE CLIMB TO THE PANTHÉON
(Le Petit Parisien, November 23, 1924)

The final arrangements for the ceremony marking the transfer of Jean Jaurès's ashes to the Panthéon began yesterday and were completed that very night. This morning, everything will be ready.

LAWS OF POPULATION FLUCTUATION
OF SEVERAL COEXISTING
SPECIES IN THE SAME AREA
BY V. VOLTERRA
(French Association for the Advancement of the Sciences, Lyon, 1926)

Let there be two species (of animals, for example). The first gets its food from its natural habitat, and, if it were alone, would grow exponentially. The second does not find food in its natural habitat, and, if it were alone, would decrease exponentially. If the second species were to eat the first, what would happen? […] The fluctuations of the number of individuals of each species are thus periodic. […]

Let us suppose some animals in each species are destroyed (by fishing). […] We see that, when the intensity of fishing grows, the number of individuals in the first species grows and the number in the second decreases, which is to say that fishing, as verified by statistics from the Adriatic, has a favorable effect before, during, and after the war.

ELECTROCUTED! A SCIENTIFIC KILLING...

(L'Humanité, special edition, August 23, 1927)

Boston, August 23, 12:30 a.m. local time. How to burn a man in an electric chair.

Madeiros was put in the chair at 12:02. He died at 12:09. Sacco was placed in the electric chair at 12:11. He died at 12:19. Vanzetti was put in the chair at 12:20. He died at 12:26.

This is not a judicial error. It is an "example."

For the proletariat, it's an open declaration of war!

THE G. CASE

BY J. MEYERBEER, PSYCHIATRIC DOCTOR,
SAINT-MAURICE HOSPITAL

(French Review of Psychiatric Medicine, Vol. 11, 1930)

Twelve years later, we return to the case of G., a former polytechnician who injured his head in combat, and who was hospitalized after having murdered his aunt, his sister, and his uncle. We refer back to our article in the *Gaz. Assoc. Psy. Doc. Fr.* (Vol. 28, 1920).

As we then reported, G. is a calm patient who is well-liked by the staff. In this short note, we revisit his relations with the outside world.

FAMILY SITUATION

G.'s oldest sister—who during the first few years visited him regularly and brought him newspapers, and, depending on the season, fruit, cakes, or chocolate—stopped visiting when she gave birth to a baby girl. Apart from the fact that the Saint-Maurice Hospital is not a place for a child, G.'s brother-in-law, a lawyer, thought that her visits could be dangerous for the little girl and thus for her mother as well. She has therefore replaced the visits with regular written correspondence. G. kindly replies to all of her letters.

CURRENT EVENTS

Apart from the epistolary exchanges with his sister, G. maintains extensive scientific correspondence with several mathematicians. He also receives periodical mathematics journals and monthly newsletters.

During our interviews, he never fails to comment on the events he knows something about. His analyses are sometimes surprising in their acuity. Of this we will give but one example, that of the transfer of Jean Jaurès's remains to the Pantheon (in 1924), which he told us represented a change of mentality, since this act established Jaurès as the war's first victim.

MATHEMATICS

We sometimes think it quite a shame that G. cannot teach mathematics, because he possesses remarkable teaching abilities, which he only has the chance to show during our interviews. We view as evidence the way he summarized an article he was reading on sardine fishing. Here are a few lines from the notes we took during this particular interview:

"Look at this, Doctor Meyerbeer, during the war, there was less fishing in the Mediterranean, of course, but in what they were catching, there were more and more sharks, in proportion, you see? Well, there's an Italian scholar who explains this with differential equations. And he proves that, the more sardines are fished, the more sardines there are in the sea."

We must confess that we have learned more about mathematics over the course of observing this patient's behavior than we did at school.

We should add that G.'s skill as a mathematician is recognized among the experts in the field. He summarizes the results of his research in articles that he then sends to specialized journals, which publish them. His articles appear to be read and used, because they are cited by several mathematicians in other articles that G. has showed us. In one of these articles, his name is associated with a theorem, "G.'s theorem"; another uses "G.'s constant." Students have even defended dissertations in which they have answered questions raised by G. in his work. He keeps us informed on the day-to-day progress of his research and mathematics in general.

We asked him if he would like to meet his mathematician correspondents—which we would have considered beneficial for this patient who has no real contact with the world—but he calmly refused, asserting his desire for peace and quiet.

THE PROBLEM OF THE TWO RACES

BY R. VON MISES, ISTANBUL

(Matematicheskii Sbornik, Moscow, 1934)

The example that follows is, by its very subject, of particular interest.

In a country in Europe whose inhabitants number around 65 million, the population is composed of two races A and B, with respective figures of 0.9% and 99.1%. A very small number of these inhabitants perform scientific research in physics or chemistry. No absolute scale to measure scientific capacity exists. It is generally accepted that the winners of the Nobel Prize form a set of the highest values with this capacity. The list of winners from the years 1901 to 1933 includes 27 names from said county, of which 5 belong to race A.

We will now address these figures with established formulas.

[…]

From these calculations, we can conclude that there is a

probability of about 85% that, among the individuals of race A, the probability of there being an eminent talent in physics or chemistry is at least 20 times and at most 42 times greater than in race B.

EXERCISES IN MULTIPLICATION AND DIVISION
(Matematisches Arbeits- und Lehrbuch, Neuenheim-Verlag, 1937)

- The construction of an insane asylum costs 6 million Reichsmarks. How many detached houses at 15,000 Reichsmarks each could have been built for that sum?
- The care of a mentally ill patient costs 8 Reichsmarks a day. How many Reichsmarks will this mentally ill patient cost after 40 years?

★

PIERRE MEYER (interview, December 18, 2006, cont.). *I'm the one who saved these two articles. But like me, Mortaufs was interested in what was happening in Germany. Bernadette told me about the little German girls with blond braids whom the family hosted during the International Exposition in 1937. There were also grand receptions in Chatou, with members of the French Academy, friends from the France-Germany Committee, sometimes foreign guests as well. Marguerite had a notebook in which she wrote down the menus for the dinners she gave. As for Mortaufs, he had been going to Germany since the early '30s—he had some scientific contacts and many friends there. He traveled a lot, I think. Marguerite didn't go with him, but with that whole household, what would you expect?*

★

CARMO'S CONJECTURE
IN THE FINITE CASE

NOTE BY A. SILBERBERG, PRESENTED BY C. MORTAUFS

(Reports from the Academy of Sciences, Meeting of March 27, 1939)

We prove, for Galois fields, a conjecture similar to the one proposed by Carmo in the complex field. From this we deduce a few corollaries and a few questions to which we hope to return in a future paper.

★

PIERRE MEYER (interview, December 18, 2006, cont.). *This is André Silberberg's very first article. It may well also be the very first note Mortaufs presented at the Academy of Sciences. He was elected at the beginning of 1939. This article was found among Mireille Duvivier's papers. The ones on Gorenstein, too. She must have gotten them from her mother.*

★

ASSESSMENT OF THE G. CASE
BY J. MEYERBEER, PSYCHIATRIC DOCTOR,
SAINT-MAURICE HOSPITAL

*(Gazette of the Association of Psychiatric
Doctors of France, Vol. 47, 1939)*

In our previous articles (*Gaz. Assoc. Psy. Doc. Fr. 28, 1920, Fr. Rev. Psy. Med. 11, 1930),* we mentioned G.'s interest in current events. Here we will be content to make a list of the subjects on which he has commented for us over the years.

TOPICS FROM CURRENT EVENTS
ADDRESSED BY THE PATIENT

Among these, the Paris Colonial Exposition of 1931, the choice of Hitler as German chancellor, the death of Paul Painlevé (a mathematician who didn't retreat from our times, he commented), the riots of February 1934, the victory of the Popular Front, the start of the war in Spain, and the Olympic Games in Berlin.

He was particularly taken aback by the interviews with Hitler published by certain newspapers. "Look, Doctor Meyerbeer, the journalist even had that fraud autograph a photo for him," he showed us one day.

In mathematics, the important step taken by a Russian mathematician towards demonstrating Goldbach's conjecture was worth several explanations. "Doctor Meyerbeer, you know what a prime number is, right?" he asked us. Of course, and the patient knows that his therapist knows what a prime number is.

MANICO-MELANCHOLICUS

The patient shifts easily, unexpectedly, and rapidly from a dejected mood to one of happy restlessness, often while speaking on the same topic. This disorder, which is rather mild, seems to particularly manifest during our conversations. The racist politics of the ruling Nazi Party in Germany seem to depress him profoundly.

"They're going to exterminate us, Doctor Meyerbeer, you and me both. You won't be able to escape," he tells us regularly in a bleak voice. And sometimes, almost without taking another breath, he bursts into laughter while showing us a mathematics article in which a Jewish German scholar calculates the probability (which is very high) of a Jewish German being better in physics than an "Aryan" German.

"But can't you see it's a joke, Doctor Meyerbeer? Don't you know I can prove the same thing about psychiatrists for you?"

We must admit that we do not always understand what makes him laugh (especially in mathematics). We considered giving him a lithium treatment, but the mildness of his disorder does not seem to hinder him, especially as we are certain that mathematics, and the fact that he can either find the subject funny or work on it seriously, is enough to bring him back to the side of euphoria.

SAID AND UNSAID

As the list above shows, for twenty years already, the patient has addressed a wide variety of subjects with us. However, it must be noted that G. has never spoken about the triple murder or his time in the war, either spontaneously or at our request. Every question concerning one of these subjects causes a brilliant and slightly exalted discourse to emerge on quite unrelated subjects.

Apart from prime numbers, sardine fishing, the scientific dispositions of Jewish Germans, current politics, and, as always, succubi and other demons with blue eyes, here are a few examples of his assertions collected over the course of the years:

"Doctor Meyerbeer, I am your Robert le Diable. Did you know that the real Robert the Devil passed himself off as a madman?"

"My mother slept with the devil."

"There is a butterfly with my name—no, not G., Robert-le-Diable."

"My sister was the one born from my mother's hideous adultery."

"I hate dogs. Because I loved a woman who preferred cats."

"I should write about you, Doctor. I would study the way you say 'perfect' every time I say something absurd."

In a feature article, currently in progress, we reveal in this case specifically (but also in several others) the connection between the murder of one's father and the phobia of dogs.

We will add that, since G. is an educated patient, he politely and carefully read our previous articles dedicated to his case. Although we thought we saw him hold back a smile, he did not make the slightest comment. Concerning an earlier version of the present article, which we had hoped would draw him out of his shell, he corrected a past participle and made this single comment: "Excuse me, but I have things to do. I have to try to answer an arithmetic problem that a mathematics student asked me about. A brilliant boy, that Silberberg! You'll hear more from him!"

★

Thus ends the last of the articles saved by Pierre Meyer in the large manila envelope.

CHAPTER IV

Strasbourg, 1939

In the large manila envelope, I had arranged—well, you may not find it very well arranged… I had saved articles from before the war that one person or another had given to me. You're handling the chronology, right? One day, if you'd like, I could relate some of the things my wife told me about that period.

....

But you wanted me to talk to you about Silberberg.

Yes, I knew him well. We were students at Strasbourg together, until 1939. Yes, both in mathematics. André had passed the exam for his teaching degree in 1938. Then he had started working on a dissertation. After a few months, he had already obtained his first result, which Henri Pariset, his professor, had called "very important." Pariset sent it to Professor Motfraus, in Paris. And Motfraus presented it to the Academy of Sciences.

No, André didn't know Motfraus personally, and for that matter, neither did I at the time. But if you don't mind, I'll speak about Motfraus at some other point.

Where was I? Oh yes, André Silberberg's note. We were both so happy! The Silberberg family even organized a little party when it was published. André's parents weren't scientists or even academics. You see, they were business owners, but their two children were in college. Yes, André did have a sister, named Clara. She died not long after the war.

No one in the family, neither Clara nor her parents, understood mathematics, but you don't need to know what a number field is to understand the honor of having an article published in a journal with your name printed underneath. I think André's father had been rather disappointed that his son hadn't tried to get into the École Polytechnique. At the party, he declared how relieved he was. And we all drank white wine on the balcony of the family apartment, overlooking the Ill River.

André was brilliant, good at everything. Very athletic. He was the goalie on our soccer team at the university. He also won the silver medal in the 800 meters at the university track championship. In 1938, I believe. He trained almost every morning at the Vauban stadium. At that time, you couldn't just go running out on the street. And he was a musician. He played the piano. You know Mozart's Fantasia? He really liked Mozart.

Yes, I was a student, too. Not as brilliant. And I had to work to pay for my schooling. Pariset suggested I work at the library of the Mathematics Institute. That way, I would earn a little money while being surrounded with books.

Here's what I wanted to tell you about. André, a few other students, and I formed a defense group. Yes, against the anti-Semites. In those years, signs that said "Forbidden to dogs and Jews" were appearing in the windows of more and more cafés and restaurants in Strasbourg. In French or German. You're a historian, you must speak German. "Juden unerwünscht," Jews are unwanted, it's more elegant… They tried, a little more each day, to apply the bans that affected Jews on the other side of the Rhine to this side as well. Since Jews were the enemies of Hitler, they were called "warmongers." A few months earlier, at the time of the Munich Agreement, there was even the start of a real pogrom against Jewish business owners. Fortunately, the shop André's parents owned (and his parents themselves) had been spared. The atmosphere was terrible. We don't have the right words to talk about that time. I'm not going to tell you the atmosphere was, I don't know, "deleterious." It seems to me that it's up to people like you to invent words. Are you recording this?

. . . .

But I wanted to tell you about our "actions." We ripped down more than one of those nauseating signs. Of course, this generally led to fights. But we were well trained. André even tried to teach me French kickboxing. We took a few serious blows now and again. One evening, we attacked the headquarters of a party pretending to be "Alsatian separatists"… needless to say, their autonomy was simply an allegiance to Nazi Germany. A real brawl followed.

But we took the most serious beating during the attack on the bookstore. Does that surprise you? It was clearly a Nazi bookstore, the Volksbuchhandlung. We broke some glass, nothing major, but that time we had a little trouble getting away. The guards were pretty burly. André got a bit scratched up. Well, I say scratched up, but it was serious enough for him to need a doctor. We called Doctor Sonntag, who was the doctor for the Silberberg family, but also a professor at the school of medicine and a personal friend of Pariset's. Have you heard of Sonntag? Sonntag sewed up what needed to be, at the hospital, but in a discreet manner. André, with his right hand bandaged up, couldn't write anything for two weeks. He was quite pleased to find piano études for the left hand.

Since I was telling you about that bookstore… I'm going to show you something. A book I snuck out with me, or rather confiscated, that day, and which by some miracle I still have. Since you read German, look at how they taught addition and subtraction in German primary schools in 1939.

....

You see: they added the areas of the territories "we" had confiscated in the "Versailler Diktat." That's what Hitler called the Treaty of Versailles. Yes, of course, you know that already. Alsace-Moselle was part of it, for 14,521.8 square kilometers. Note the "point 8." There are other square kilometers, with decimal points, in Belgium, Denmark, Lithuania, Czechoslovakia, without forgetting Danzig, and especially Poland. It's very instructive: a big sum, with decimal points. And look at this one: subtraction, now. Before the war, the Reich's territory was 542,622 square kilometers. You have to find the total area before 1938. Yes, they stop in 1938 because, by then, the conquest had already started, thanks to the Anschluss and the Sudetes. The book dates from 1939. Ah! The blue notebook. No, don't take notes, it's not worth it: if you want to look at the textbook in more detail, I'll let you borrow it. There's a whole series of exercises like this.

But I was talking to you about André Silberberg. Didn't you say you did some research in the Heinrich Kürz archives at the University of N.? Did you know that he came to Strasbourg, precisely in 1939? Yes, Kürz. And that he had a discussion with André Silberberg? Let me tell you about that. He came to speak at Pariset's seminar. He was an important guest; Pariset had promoted the talk in his class and invited all the students to come listen. So I went along with André. Kürz had just proven, I can no longer remember what exactly, but it was something very important in number theory. It was actually Motfraus who had invited him to give a series of lectures in Paris, and Kürz was stopping in Strasbourg on his way back. He was the Vice-Rektor of his university, you know, and for us there was no doubt he was a Nazi. Otherwise he wouldn't have been appointed Vice-Rektor. I suppose Pariset went to pick him up at the station. What I remember perfectly is that they arrived together. I can still see them climbing up the monumental stairs at the entrance to the university. And I can still hear them, especially Kürz, who was speaking very loudly, and in German. Pariset was content to nod in agreement.

André and I, in fact our whole generation, learned French at school. German was our mother tongue, the language we spoke at home. A lecture in German was no problem. Besides, I should say that Kürz was an excellent speaker and his lecture was fascinating. Even so, let's just say he was perhaps a little too smug. At the end, there was applause, one or two questions, and then people started standing up and speaking amongst themselves. Pariset introduced André to Kürz: "As you may know, this is the brilliant young man who proved that…" But Kürz knew: "Ah! It's you! Excellent work! They told me about you at the Academy of Sciences, where I was invited last week." The professors then went to have a beer in a nearby brasserie. Pariset kindly invited André to come along with them. Of course, the other students weren't invited. So I didn't go. But the very next afternoon, André came to tell me what happened.

It was a Tuesday; the seminar was always on Tuesdays. At the end of the month of May, if I remember correctly. I should be able to find the exact date for you, if you're interested. It was a beautiful late afternoon, almost a summer evening, that I can remember. So they went in the café, where there was another group of professors, historians, already sitting at a table with their steins of beer. It was the closest café to the Palais Universitaire, you always saw lots of professors there. I think it still exists. How well do you know Strasbourg?

In any case, this café wasn't displaying the notorious "Forbidden to Jews" sign. They all ordered beers. André told me that Kürz had mainly talked about his life, with a bit of complacency and not much tact. He said he had enlisted in the navy at age seventeen and had been very happy to wage war. This was the war of '14. That experience had been beneficial for his health and had taught him a lot. To say this to a group of Frenchmen, in Strasbourg, in 1939, was rather provocative. André found it all very tiresome. Kürz told them about his trip to Paris, and how there had been lots of people who came to listen to his lectures. He spoke of the way peace and Franco-German friendship had been celebrated in a walk with Professor Motfraus in the Jardin des Tuileries. Kürz even went as far as to proclaim how happy he was, as a German, to find himself here in Strasbourg. While gesturing to the Palais Universitaire, a Wilhelminian building, through the café windows, he said, "You French cannot understand—this is the true German spirit." And he added: "We will return." The atmosphere was tense, André told me. At the table next to them, the historians went quiet. The mathematicians didn't say a word, out of politeness or embarrassment, and that had irritated André a little. But, as a student invited to a table of professors, what could he do?

He had described all this to me rather gravely, but it made him laugh as well. André was like that. Very serious and very funny at the same time.

He was my friend.

André had a great sense of humor. I think he was rather pleased with himself that day. He had quite simply asked a mathematical question. Quite simply, he repeated to me. A real, serious question. But in French. Politely, but in a loud, clear voice. Over at the table of historians, he saw the one facing him smile slightly. Kürz thought for a moment, shook his head, and gave his answer: "Ich weiss nicht," I don't know, in German. "I might know," André said, and he added politely, in French: "I should like to write to you, Professor. I will send you my proof as soon as I've worked out the details." After which, they all got up, I guess Pariset was the one who paid the bill, and they parted ways.

Would you like more coffee?

I'm sure you know the name Daniel Roth. Yes, he was one of your colleagues, a historian. But he was interested in the Renaissance. You may also have heard of Marcel Schmitt. Yes? Of course, you know all the historians. He was a professor at the University of Strasbourg as well. He wrote a little book about his memories, he talks about Roth in it. You've read it? Why am I talking about Roth? Because he and Schmitt were among the group of historians at the café. The one who smiled at hearing André speak French, that was Roth. The historian with the smile, André had said to me. He was smiling, too, when he told me about it. Daniel Roth caught up with him, in front of the statue of Goethe, right in front of the university, and congratulated him on his question. They walked together for a little while. André was in awe; as you know, at that time, relationships between professors and students were rather distant. Roth was already quite famous, and André was just a student. Yet Roth knew André's name. He had heard about our raid on the bookstore, only because Doctor Sonntag was his cousin and had told him about it. André tried to explain the question he had asked Kürz. But the great man knew nothing about class field theory, which really made André laugh. And then they spoke about hell, and the situation in Germany.

In Strasbourg, we were very close to Germany; there were a lot of German refugees, so we knew what was going on. In particular, as students, we had heard people talking about what was happening within the universities. Living one day at a time, the anxiety whenever a political topic came up in conversation, the *Horst-Wessel-Lied* sung in unison with one arm raised, Party membership, the class boycotts, the dismissal of undesirables. Yes, of course, you know all that, that's your job. You'll know this as well: in 1939, there was no doubt about it, we knew there would be war. Like André, like us all, Roth knew that the German had been right and that they were going to return, like he had said, to take back their square kilometers of vital space, and that they would do here what they had already done there.

Roth and André parted and went their separate ways, each to his own abode.

The next morning, Daniel Roth had a copy of Dante's *Inferno* brought to André. He had dedicated and signed the book. André was very proud of it. He brought it to the library to show me. Later on, he lent it to one of his friends, right before he was arrested. It's too bad you couldn't have met Mireille Duvivier. I'll tell you her story another time.

Now I'm the one who owns the book. I'm going to show you the dedication.

Look what Daniel Roth wrote: "Absurd or not, make no mistake, the hell they're preparing for us is very well organized."

CHAPTER V

Journal of Heinrich Kürz[1]

(PARIS, 1942)

Very well organized, my trip. Left for Paris at midnight on May 28.[2] Unfortunately could not stop by Neuenbach to kiss Lotte and her mother. In the train compartment, spoke with a lieutenant who was returning from the Eastern front. Described the losses suffered. Amputations of frozen limbs. Thought of Otto Zach.[3] What a loss it would be, for science and for Germany, if he didn't come back. At least he will have done what he wanted to do, right to the end.

---

1   The mathematician and German officer Heinrich Kürz (1897-1965) kept this journal during one of his stays in Paris, then carefully typed it up. This is a translation of the journal with annotations and commentary. The document (fifteen typed pages) can be found in the Kürz Collection in the University of N. Archives. Dr. Hermann Raffke, the curator of the archives, and Dr. Bernhardt Hermann, grandson of Heinrich Kürz, gave their permission for this publication. I would like to take this opportunity to thank them.

2   The goal of Kürz's trip was to look for French mathematicians who would agree to contribute articles to the German mathematical review journal..

3   At the request of Dr. Hermann and out of consideration for potential beneficiaries, the majority of the names of the people mentioned here have been changed. The name of Otto Zach used here designates a young mathematician (1913-1943) who was both a brilliant academic and a very active member of the National Socialist Party.

May 29, 1942

In Paris, at the Hotel Raphael, between the Arc de Triomphe and
the Trocadéro. Beautiful room. Antique woodwork.[4] Met Jünger,
the famous writer and hero of the Great War, who is staying in the
next room over and wanted to know what a mathematician like
me was doing in Paris working as a member of the occupation
forces. Explained to him how a review journal works and our need
for contributions from French mathematicians. Walked together
from the Trocadéro to the Étoile and back. Had a beer together on
a café terrace. Atmosphere was cheerful and Parisian. "So, you're
a salesman for German science," he said to me.

Seeing Jünger gave me the idea of keeping a journal to make
note of what I'm doing over the next few days in Paris.[5]

May 30, 1942

Between 2 and 4 in the morning, heard British planes, bombs not
very far from here, dropped on the Renault factories. That's what
I call an act of terrorism.

There's a big mirror in the hotel room. I think I look rather
handsome in my uniform. One of the advantages of the war.

Visited Yersin, whom I met ten years ago when he came to

---

4   The officers of the occupation forces were housed in luxurious hotels in the
beautiful neighborhoods in the west of Paris.

5   The writer Ernst Jünger (1895-1995), who was a captain with the German
military staff, was indeed living at the Hotel Raphael. It should be noted that he
was the youngest recipient of the Prussian *Pour le Mérite* award in 1918. Although
there is no material evidence, it seems rather certain that Kürz rewrote his text,
at least in part, after Jünger's *Parisian Journals* were published in 1949. See notes
13 and 43.

study with Xanten. Tense atmosphere. Proposed he contribute to the review journal: his expertise in geometry would be very useful to us. He didn't give me an outright no, but didn't show much enthusiasm, either. For that matter, he hardly said anything. I gave him some food tickets, for his elderly father—I hope that will help convince him.[6]

Morstauf came to the Raphael while I was away.[7] I think I'll see him on Monday. He left me some reading material: two French newspapers (*La Gerbe* and *Je suis partout*[8]) and a letter.

May 31, 1942

Sunday morning. Thought of Otto Zach again. Where is he exactly, and in what condition? This is a time when many brave men will go through the gates of hell—and many will have seen it even before their own deaths.

Walked across Paris to the Abwehr headquarters at the Hotel

---

6 Catherine Billotte, daughter of Claude Yersin (1904-1997) stated (Interview, December 5, 2008) that her grandfather saved these tickets; he never used them. She added that her father had never criticized Morstauf's attitude during the occupation, undoubtedly because of Morstauf's status as a "broken face." On this subject, she mentioned the trip Yersin had made with his own father near the front, even before the 1918 armistice occurred (Yersin was fourteen years old), in order to identify the body of one of his uncles.

7 The mathematicians Christian Morstauf (1893-1996) and Heinrich Kürz had maintained a relationship as both scientists and friends ever since Morstauf's trip to N. in 1932. They wrote each other many letters, which are held in Kürz's Nachlass (collection) at the University of N. archives. From the start of the war, Kürz went to Paris several times, which means that he and Morstauf must have seen each other quite regularly.

8 *La Gerbe* (*The Sheaf*) and *Je suis partout* (*I Am Everywhere*) were French collaborationist newspapers.

Lutetia, where Blank,[9] one of my friends from Gymnasium, is assigned, and where they even work on Sundays. Had a drink with him. Then, on Boulevard Saint-Michel, I contemplated the fountain's archangel while thinking of it as a symbol of our victory and the peace that will follow.

Had dinner with Wallerant at a rather popular restaurant, Le Mahieu.[10] We traded news with each other, in particular of Sir Michael Vendall, who was evacuated from London to Bangor, Wales, with his students, so he gets to keep on phlegmatically playing bridge while our compatriots are killed by the bombs dropped by his.[11] Wallerant spoke to me about a conference at Cambridge, just before the war, in which Xanten had taken part, and how he had seemed so happy to finally be back in front of a chalkboard. "It was almost pathetic. A man so lively, so brilliant, how could you have kept him from teaching his classes?" he asked me; but Xanten is dead and that question has become useless. At least he died of an illness, and before the war.

Fortunately, Wallerant doesn't seem to know that Ulrich and his wife committed suicide, or in any case, he didn't mention it. It's a cruel but essential battle we're fighting, and casualties are inevitable.[12]

9　This friend also appears in Kürz's letters, sometimes under the name of Leutnant Blank, sometimes under that of Doktor Blank.

10　Le Mahieu occupied the southernmost corner of Rue Soufflot and Boulevard Saint-Michel.

11　Fernand Wallerant (1890-1953) and (Sir) Michael Vendall (1889-1960) were both specialists in number theory like Kürz and Morstauf, one a professor at the Sorbonne and the other at University College London.

12　The German mathematicians Edmund Xanten (1880-1938) and Friedrich Ulrich (1870-1942) were both victims of the Nazi anti-Semitic laws. Xanten

Told him about my trip to Padua, spring in Italy. It pleased me to say I received the doctoral degree *honoris causa*. Wallerant is probably going to agree to help us: he needs a *laissez-passer* document for his wife, and I advised him to go see Blank.

June 1, 1942

Each morning, I have a café crème and three croissants brought up to my room, along with the *Pariser Zeitung*, in order to immerse myself in the Parisian atmosphere. I listen to Radio Paris in order to improve my French. I also read *Je suis partout*, the newspaper Morstauf brought me. The book reviews are quite spirited. There's also information about the enemies of Germany and the false names they're using.

Yesterday, I tried to get news about Gorenstein, a Jewish mathematician who has long been shut away in a lunatic asylum, but Wallerant didn't know anything. I never forget the fact that there are people in this world more unfortunate than I.[13]

Spent the day working in my room while waiting for news from Morstauf. Tried once more to understand how Silberberg could really prove that lemma he sent me three years ago, after our discussion in Strasbourg. I can prove it up to dimension 41, but no more. I'm sure he doesn't know how to do it either. Typical Jewish

---

was not dismissed from his post immediately in 1933 (because he had fought in World War I), but Nazi students (among whom was the young Otto Zach) organized a boycott of his courses and he was forced to stop teaching. Ulrich and his wife committed suicide at the beginning of 1942 to avoid being deported.

13   The mention of "more unfortunate" people, which seems a little artificial here, may have been copied from Jünger. On the French mathematician Robert Gorenstein (1893-1949), see note 42.

behavior. But I might have found something else, with the help of a theorem that was just published by another French mathematician.

Received a short note from Yersin's father, who thanks me for the tickets. Nothing more.[14]

June 2, 1942

Morstauf came by to look for me at the Raphael after lunch. Still doing very well and rather good-looking, in spite of the leather mask, especially with that elegant red lock of hair.

He couldn't come yesterday, which was Monday, because of the meeting at the Academy of Sciences. We walked while he told me about the Academy. He apologized for not being able to invite me this time; he said the meetings have become more secret. According to him, there's still a lot to do in order to return the Academy to the true friends of science. He started getting agitated as he told me about a note published by Nadault. This physicist is under house arrest in a place where he cannot perform experiments, so he's started working in mathematics, specifically in probability theory. What shocks Morstauf is that the Academy has agreed to publish his notes.[15] At least, he says, as of last fall nothing Jewish has been published. He added that Nadault isn't Jewish, but his daughter married a Jewish physicist, who had to be executed by firing squad not too long ago. He also told me that he himself tried

---

14   Kürz saved this short note from Yersin (University of N. archives).

15   The physicist Émile Nadault (1870-1947) had been a public supporter of the Popular Front. He was arrested by the Germans in October 1940, then released. At the time of Kürz's visit to Paris, he had been put on house arrest in Chartres.

to have a Jewish member of the French Academy, who has settled quite peacefully in the United States, expelled from the group, arguing that he doesn't come to meetings, but no one followed up, under the pretext that it's not the Academy's custom. It's a venerable institution; they need a little time to adapt to new ideas. "And you know," he said, "at the end of this academic year, at the CNRS,* the Jewish question will be resolved: there won't be a single Jew left."

They do have a bit more difficulty here with the so-called international institutions. For example, Morstauf told me about the International Time Bureau at the Paris Observatory, where they haven't been able to expel undesirables, and he mentioned the name of a Jewish astronomer who is still peacefully presiding there.[16]

I proposed we go to the library of the Henri Poincaré Institute, on Rue Pierre-Curie, but as soon as we got there, someone at the door told us that the librarian had just left and we couldn't go in. This probably wasn't true. It seems to me this kind of thing needs to be made more rational.

After leaving Morstauf, I walked down Rue Saint-Jacques, with the length of the Lycée Louis-le-Grand on my right and the Sorbonne on my left. I bought an unpaired volume from the complete works of Lagrange at a used bookstore, then I lost myself in a sort of labyrinth of little streets; one of them happened to be named after Lagrange, and another after Dante, with no street running parallel or perpendicular to any of the others. This, too, could be

---

*   Centre national de la recherche scientifique (French National Center for Scientific Research) (Trans.)

16   This is probably Maurice Fried (1895-1943). He was arrested in July 1942 and deported to Auschwitz where he disappeared in December 1943.

made more rational. But that is our role here, and I have no doubt that we will succeed.

The lemma I came up with seems to work.

June 3, 1942

Today, Morstauf organized a meeting in a café on Rue Claude-Bernard. He teaches everywhere: at the Sorbonne, the École Polytechnique, the École Normale Supérieure.[17] He was supposed to bring students from the École Normale Supérieure so that we could convince them to work for us, but he arrived on his own. "The students are coming," he told me.

He launched into one of his usual lengthy monologues, mixed with his recollections from the ceremony for my university's two hundred fiftieth anniversary, which he attended five years ago,[18] his childhood memories, and his political opinions. He also mentioned, as he did three years ago in the Jardin des Tuileries, the cemetery of N., his love of peace, Germany and its power—because France's future rests in that power—the memory of all the colleagues he had met there, and even a dog (Tiedemann's, if I understood correctly) that had reminded him of his childhood in the heart of Africa. He told me about a river, the Saloum, and its delta, and of course from there he arrived at the war, the great war, along with the military cemetery where his brother is buried,

---

17   In fact, Morstauf held several teaching positions concurrently. This practice has become rare, but was still rather common at the time. For example, during the 1930s, Paul de Saint-Bonnet had concurrent positions at the Sorbonne, the École Normale Supérieure, the École Centrale, and the École des Mines.

18   The University of N. celebrated this anniversary in 1937 with grand Nazi pomp. Morstauf was among the foreigners invited to the ceremony.

in Brittany, I believe, and of course his injury, which he refers to as a second birth. Then he told me about Saint-Bonnet, "his master" who had given him a lot of support ever since the time his injury, but who died last winter, at a very old age.[19]

For all that, the students never came; Morstauf flew into a terrible rage against the school's assistant director, a physicist and enemy of Germany, who he claims pits the students against us.[20] His fits of rage are well known among mathematicians. As for me, I lost my whole day.

In the evening, my friend from the Lutetia took me to a brothel near the Palais-Royal. There's another advantage to the war! The establishment is reserved for officers. The girls are clean and friendly, and they understand German well enough to do what's asked of them. They had a piano there; one of the girls was plinking out *Für Elise* on it. At first I thought of taking her place, but I felt a Beethoven sonata would be poorly suited to the locale, so I didn't do anything.[21]

June 4, 1942

Morstauf again today. He took me to the German Institute, on Rue Saint-Dominique near Les Invalides, one of the nicer walks. On the way, he tried to say a few words to me in German, but he's made hardly any progress since my last trip in December 1940. Still, he managed to say:

19　On the mathematician Paul de Saint-Bonnet, see notes 17 and 32.

20　Student testimonials from the period mention Morstauf's collaborationist proselytism during his courses at the École Normale Supérieure.

21　Heinrich Kürz was a professional-grade pianist.

Wie weh wird mir
Wie brennt meine alte Wunde!

I pretended not to recognize that it was a quotation, especially because it came from a Jewish writer.[22] At the Institute, I went over to greet the director, Doktor Epting. There were lots of people there, mainly lots of French people: writers, musicians, and actors; pretty women, starlets, and songstresses. The discussion, an animated one, was about a very interesting trip the actors took to Berlin a few months ago,[23] then about the Arno Breker exposition at the Orangerie. "Have you read Cocteau's article?" someone asked.[24] "Ah, those Aryan athletes are so handsome," a woman said. "But that's the true German spirit!" a man exclaimed. Morstauf introduced him to me; he's a chemist by the name of Ollier, a handsome man with a long, serious face.[25] There was also an inventor, Georges C., who thinks he's the greatest living French savant (Morstauf warned me we would meet him, and said Georges C. is very sensitive on this point). Georges C. recognized me despite my uniform; he said he remembered my

22 The writer and poet of the verses quoted by Morstauf is Heinrich Heine (1797-1856), whose books were burned in the public squares of German cities in 1933. The two verses can be translated literally as "How I suffer / How my old injury burns me."

23 A group of French actors were invited to Berlin in March 1942. See also note 35.

24 A grand exhibition was showing the works of Arno Breker (1900-1991), the official sculptor of the Third Reich, at the Musée de l'Orangerie in the Jardin des Tuileries. Kürz doesn't seem to have gone to it during this trip. The article "Salut à Breker" (Salute to Breker), by the writer Jean Cocteau, had appeared in the weekly collaborationist magazine *Comœdia* on May 23.

25 Like Morstauf, Ollier was a member of the Groupe Collaboration.

trip to the Academy of Sciences right before the war. Morstauf congratulated him on a speech he made that was broadcast on Radio Paris a few days ago.

"You knew," Morstauf said to him, "how to touch the hearts of the French people by communicating the depth of your attachment to Hitler."

"Ah! That's because I'm not a convert," he answered.

To tell the truth, this man and his intensity frightened me a little.[26] "Your article on French science was very good," Morstauf said to Ollier.[27]

Morstauf's relations with Georges C. and Ollier seemed slightly tense. They're probably all jealous of each other, trying to see whose love of Germany will bring the most fame or more materials. He introduced me to another man whose name I didn't catch, and who congratulated me on our conquering force, capable of assuring a race's hegemony. "Ah!" interrupted Morstauf, "what we want is a France where order, work, and hierarchy prevail."

"But it's been led for so long by immigrants, Jewry, and Freemasonry," the other chided.

Later, Morstauf told me that this man dreams of becoming a government minister. He also said that he himself was approached by Abel Bonnard to direct a new Franco-European cultural center.

---

26   The fanaticism of the scientist here called Georges C. (1870-1960) would lead him, a few weeks later, to "give his whole self to Hitler" by biting a cyanide capsule in public, which he survived.

27   This is probably in reference to an article titled "Le professeur Ollier nous dit" ("Professor Ollier Tells Us") which appeared in the evening edition of *Les Nouveaux Temps* on May 29, 1942.

The symbol of his broken face in the service of peace would be rather striking.[28]

June 5, 1942

Mathematical work and walks around Paris. Went to the Rive Gauche Buchhandlung, a bookstore very well placed on Boulevard Saint-Michel, at the corner of Place de la Sorbonne, with its pretty windows. Our soldiers can find things to read there and our university libraries can get what they need. A French writer, a tall blond man with black-rimmed glasses who was missing one arm, was signing his books. Probably another wounded soldier from the last war. Lots of them have sided with peace.[29]

In the evening, dinner at Morstauf's place in Chatou. I managed to find a car and get a solider to drive me there. Morstauf makes the journey by train almost daily. Since he has to be back before the curfew, his days in Paris are rather short. Huge house right on the Seine, well-kept garden. My rosebushes must also be in bloom. The whole family was assembled in my honor. Morstauf has five daughters and one son, born between 1918 and 1924, whom he presented to me one by one, from the oldest, there with her doctor husband and expecting her first child, all the way down

---

28   Starting in the 1930s, the veterans of World War I on both the French and the German side were called on to help with Nazi German propaganda, such as during the creation of the France-Germany Committee, which the Groupe Collaboration took over during the Occupation. Abel Bonnard (1883-1968), who had been the Minister of National Education and Youth since April 1942, was an active member of the Groupe Collaboration.

29   It has not been possible to identify this writer. On the exploitation of the "*gueules cassées*," or "broken faces," see previous note.

to the youngest, the only boy, who is 18 and is preparing for the École Normale Supérieure entrance exam. Morstauf would have preferred the Polytechnique, but the boy likes biology. Marguerite Morstauf, the lady of the house, has hardly changed since 1939 (I hadn't seen her since then). She's a stout woman who doesn't seem very happy but takes care of absolutely everything. What would we be without our wives? She showed me the notebook in which she writes down the menus for the dinners she gives, opened to the page corresponding to my last visit, for which there had been saddle of lamb with chilled fruit for dessert, and in the margin, she had written "*dîner épatamment réussi*"[30] (I didn't recognize that adverb). The dinner was quite a success this time as well, in spite of the restrictions.[31] "My wife's father was a well-known Catholic poet," Morstauf had told me in 1939, "named Albert Janvier." At the time, I didn't dare say I hadn't heard of him. But I've learned about him since. They're a respectable family. Madame Morstauf was a cousin of Saint-Bonnet's.[32] The children are well raised and speak German adequately. They're very Catholic. We even said grace before and after dinner.

After the meal, we smoked our pipes under a linden tree. In

---

30 In French in the original text.

31 The Morstaufs had a rather high income, resulting in part from the multiple positions mentioned in note 17, but mainly from Marguerite Morstauf's fortune inherited from her parents. This affluence and their property in Normandy surely allowed them to procure foods from the black market without difficulty.

32 Paul de Saint-Bonnet (1870-1941), a mathematician who specialized in differential equations and a member of the Academy of Sciences and the French Academy, was a first cousin to Madeleine Janvier (1871-1933), the wife of the poet Albert Janvier (1860-1910).

addition to butter and sugar, I had brought a provision of tobacco that I gave them.[33] Morstauf talked to me about the arrival of the Staatsoper in Paris last year and the French soprano Germaine Lubin as Isolde, surrounded by all those German artists.[34] He said it was the collaboration in action. He had listened to *Tristan* on the radio because of the curfew. The next time I come to Paris, I'll try to take him to the opera. We discussed his upcoming trip to Germany, specifically to Berlin and maybe N. Last fall, a whole group of French writers came to Weimar, then there were musicians in Vienna, and those actors we met yesterday at the German Institute who were in Berlin in March. Why don't you organize a trip like that for scientists, he asked me?[35] Our administration certainly has some bureaucratic red tape, but I'm hopeful that the matter of his invitation, which has been dragging on since the war started, will soon be resolved: it's already been a year since he went to Vichy to ask for all the official authorizations.

In the car on the way back, my mind wandered to genetics. The father has brown eyes, the mother has blue eyes, the six children have blue eyes. I tried to remember the children's names: Thérèse was the oldest, there was a Bernadette… Ignace was the boy (their

---

33 Tobacco was rationed in Germany starting in February 1942. As his letters indicate, Kürz had a rather sizeable reserve of it, which he had procured during a trip to Holland a few months earlier.

34 The Staatsoper (Berlin State Opera) had given performances, notably of Wagner's *Tristan and Isolde*, a year before, on May 22, 1941, for an audience of German officers, under the direction of the young conductor Herbert von Karajan (1908-1989). These performances, broadcast by Radio Paris, were a huge success.

35 German propaganda had organized trips for groups of French musicians, painters, writers, and actors, but not one for scientists.

names were all very Catholic), there was also a Marie. But the two others? I asked myself the kinds of questions you ask when you've had a little too much to drink. If they'd had a son first, would they have had six children? If they'd had a sixth daughter, would they have had a seventh child? Did he fly into one of his famous fits of rage every time his wife gave birth to another daughter? I also thought about the fact that Morstauf, who's just three years older than I am, will soon be a grandfather, while my Charlotte is only fifteen.

June 6, 1942

I went to Ranvier's on Rue du Vieux-Colombier.[36] I found him in the company of a short, lively man with round glasses. Neither one seemed delighted at my arrival. The man, whom Ranvier called François, thanked Ranvier for his article, said "Don't make a fuss over me, I'm leaving," and dashed off with his arms full of papers. It was only when he left that Ranvier apologized for not having introduced us. Too bad: that François must have been a mathematician, I could have recruited him.[37]

Ranvier suggested we go to a café on Place Saint-Sulpice. It was there, on the terrace, that we met up with Quesnay.[38] Ranvier and

---

36   Gabriel Ranvier (1906-1978) was an assistant professor of mathematics at the Sorbonne.

37   This could have been François Le Lionnais, who, besides his activities as a member of the Resistance, was researching articles for a book on mathematics that would appear after the war.

38   The mathematician Pierre Quesnay (1910-1960) was teaching at the Sorbonne. His brother René (1914-1955) was a historian, a reputed specialist in the resistance to Romanization.

Quesnay are already working on our journal, and I was hoping that they were planning to recruit new reviewers as well. But Quesnay's brother has been a prisoner for two years now and Quesnay is very disappointed that, despite his collaboration with us, his brother has still not been freed. I reminded him of the steps I've taken to help his brother get books on the Roman Empire. Quesnay didn't deny that his brother's situation has improved. Then Quesnay said he had another meeting and left. He may have been telling the truth.

In a one-on-one with Ranvier, we spoke about the contacts we'd made during my trip in the spring of '39. He remembered how I had gone through Strasbourg on my way back and asked me how the seminar there had gone. I got the impression he'd already heard what happened and just wanted to hear how I was going to tell the story about the discussion with Silberberg, so I asked what had become of that little brat.[39] I acted like I didn't know his name and described him as "the tall Jew who worked with Pariset." Obviously, Ranvier knew who I meant. Ranvier thinks Silberberg is still with the other Strasbourgers at Clermont-Ferrand, where he saw him last year, and is still working with Pariset.[40] He told me Silberberg recently published two notes in *Comptes*

---

39   The Kürz collection at the University of N. contains a letter (mathematical in nature) from André Silberberg and some official reports on a trip Kürz took to Strasbourg in Mary 1939, during which he met Silberberg and had a discussion with him. Silberberg had declared that he knew how to prove a "fundamental" lemma, which Kürz did not manage to prove until after the war.

40   The town of Strasbourg was evacuated in September 1939, and its university withdrew to Clermont-Ferrand. Many students returned home after the Reich annexed Alsace in 1940 (after being blackmailed by the Nazi authorities). The university remained at Clermont-Ferrand, despite the threats and the creation of a "Reichsuniversität" in Strasbourg.

rendus, one in December 1941 and the other a few weeks ago. I was surprised to hear that the Academy of Sciences is still publishing articles signed with a name like Silberberg.[41] They're not under his name, Ranvier said, but he refused to say any more.[42] If I want to know, it's not difficult, I just need to look in *Comptes rendus*, which doesn't have that many articles on number theory, so I should be able to easily recognize his research. Maybe he even talks about his famous lemma. It would be even simpler to ask Morstauf, but maybe he doesn't know about it. Still, it's strange I didn't notice those articles.

June 7, 1942

Sunday again. Stopped to buy a few flowers from a stall on Boulevard Saint-Michel. Was taken aback by the gaze of the sales girl, who was looking at me with immense hatred—the pupils in her blue eyes were completely retracted.[43] In thinking back on Morstauf's students, for whom we waited in vain the other day,

---

41   In conformity with the recommendations of the Occupation authorities and going beyond the letter of Vichy's anti-Semite laws, scientific journals in the Occupied Zone eliminated all Jewish authors starting in the fall of 1941.

42   During this period, some French Jewish scientists published under pseudonyms, while others used another person's name. One of the best known cases is that of Robert Gorenstein, who, though he was shut away in a psychiatric hospital, understood the significance of the first French anti-Semite laws and, starting in October 1940, changed his name on the articles he wrote to René Monod (then quickly went back to writing under his own name starting in September 1944). André Silberberg (1914-1945), mentioned here, used the pseudonym André Danglars.

43   This mention of the girl's gaze appears word-for-word in Jünger's journal. It is possible that one of the two had this meeting, then they spoke to each other about it and the other attributed it to himself.

I'm not sure whether we've really known how to touch the hearts of the French, no matter what Georges C. says.

Starting today, Jews must wear the yellow star here as well. I wonder if this rule applies in a lunatic asylum. Of course I'm thinking about Gorenstein. They've done right to keep them from publishing. It would be too complicated, putting a star on articles written by star wearers. Yet if Silberberg is still managing to get his articles published… Again I think of Zach, over there in the east, who's so good at recognizing Jewish mathematics and separating them from our Deutsche Mathematik. In any case, even in Russia, the winter must be over.

June 8, 1942

Assessment of these past few days in Paris: spent far too much time with Morstauf—I'm starting to get tired of his prayers and outpourings of love. He hardly spoke to me at all about mathematics. I wonder if he's even working on anything.

Even so, huge difficulties in establishing contact with other colleagues.

But I still proved something, in the end. The little free time I've had here has been well spent. In Berlin, I never would've managed it. Ah! How far we are from that time, just six or seven years ago, when it was so easy to work. Especially since there were so few students at the university that we could devote all of our time to our research.

My last day. Today in Paris, tomorrow in Berlin. Had my breakfast in the Raphael's restaurant. While there, met a Lieutenant Müller.[44]

---

44 Because this lieutenant had a very common name, it is hard to identify him. His view of numbers, also very common, does not help in determining

Unlike the majority of the hotel's inhabitants, he doesn't work for the MBF[45] at the Majestic Hotel, but on Avenue Foch, with the Gestapo, dealing with the Jewish question. His work consists of filling the trains being sent to Upper Silesia with Jews. He's very proud to have come up with the idea of taking Jews who were arrested as terrorists and deporting them for being Jewish: no one is keeping count of the so-called "members of the Resistance" who've been imprisoned or deported. The convoys of Jews must each contain a thousand individuals. He was surprised to discover I'm a specialist in number theory. To be more exact, he was surprised that something called number theory exists. He explained his view of numbers, which is pragmatic and extremely precise. For him, the idea of "a thousand or so," for example, doesn't exist. What exists is 1,000, pure and simple.

In our century, systematic men like him will be the ones who make history, and they'll be the ones we remember, perhaps.[46]

who he is.

45 Militärbefehlshaber in Frankreich: German military command in France.

46 Kürz saved his train tickets. We therefore know that he indeed left Paris on June 8. Contrary to what is written here, he did not go straight back to Berlin, but went via N., where he stopped for at least one day, two or three perhaps.

CHAPTER VI

The Form of a City

(N., 1943–2005)

Perhaps a shade of yellow, the little mutt looks grayish in the black and white photograph. The circumstances this image evokes (the season, the presence of several people, the special attention two of them are giving the dog) explains its cheerful air. The rhododendron bush, at the far left, is in bloom. It is summer. The left hand of one of the two men seated on the wooden bench pets the dog's head resting on his neighbor's thigh. Both of them have pipes in their mouths. To their right—that is, on the left side of the photograph—between the bench and the rhododendron, five people are seated in metal chairs around a garden table.

Where was this garden? One must open the map of the little town of N., sixty-two years after this photograph was taken.

On the map, the train station can be identified right away, thanks to the thick black lines of the rails superimposed on the bright colors used by the illustrator. The eye then distinguishes the river (blue) and the bridge, the town center, with its main square and pedestrian streets, and finally a neighborhood of individual houses surrounded by gardens. A soft shade of green has been chosen to represent this neighborhood. It is situated near the town center, but far enough from the railroad tracks that the noise and other disturbances from convoys going east (or west) would not be perceived. The streets in this neighborhood are all named after famous German scientists, philosophers, or writers (Bunsen, Gauss, Kant, Spankerfel, Humboldt, Riemann, Schiller…).

Going clockwise around the metal openwork table, one sees a teenage girl, then two men and two women, all four middle-aged. All of them are looking towards the camera, which means that some of them (the girl and one of the women) had to turn towards the photographer. Between the girl and this woman, in the foreground, is an empty chair. A clay tobacco jar has been placed at the center of the table. The men have drinking glasses in front of them. The man sitting nearest to the girl is in the middle of serving himself from a near-empty bottle. His hand obscures the label, but the contents are almost certainly a pale-colored spirit, which could be kirsch.

To the right of the actual map (2005 edition) are five pictures (numbered and captioned) of places deemed by the little town's tourist center as particularly interesting for visitors. The numbers on these pictures correspond to other (identical) numbers on the map itself. One of these places, the one marked with the number 4, is a pastry shop. Founded in 1858 (according to the caption), Korb & Schlag is located in a pink gabled house, with geraniums brightening up its windows, on the north side of the marketplace (Marktplatz), as shown in the photo.

A careful handwritten inscription (in German) on the back of the photograph identifies the seven people and the dog. The place (Humboldtstrasse, N.) and the date (July 6, 1943) are also indicated. The dog is named Stefi (a diminutive of Stefanie, which tells us the dog was female). The teenage girl is Charlotte Kürz, daughter of the mathematician Heinrich Kürz. Two light blonde braids tied with white ribbons frame her young face, which is a little large for her body. She is dressed in a dark skirt, white socks, and a white short-sleeved blouse, with a dark neckerchief worn as a tie and tightened at the neck with a braided leather kerchief slide. Her head is slightly tilted and she is smiling at the camera.

Picture number 1 shows a fountain located in the middle of the Marktplatz. The fountain bears the name Gretchen am Spinnrade, or "Margaret at the spinning wheel," because of the little statue at the top that indeed represents a girl working at her spinning wheel. As the tourist center's commentary explains, according to an old tradition, before passing their exams or leaving for the army, the students of the University of N. must climb the fountain to plant a kiss on little Gretchen's stone lips.

The girl in the photo is no more than fifteen or sixteen years old. The other individuals are all much older. The two men seated at the table, according to the inscription on the back, are Doktor (medical) Friedrich (the one pouring himself a drink) and Professor-Doktor von Apfeldorf. Both wear dark suit jackets, white collared shirts, and ties. Around von Apfeldorf's left arm is an armband bearing a swastika. Behind them, one can distinguish the wall of a house and a window with a white frilled curtain and wooden shutters.

Number 2 on the map is Gustav-August University, founded in

1687 by Prince Gustav August and host to many renowned scholars since that time. The description is followed by a list of these scholars, in which one can recognize the names of the streets in the neighborhood where the 1943 photo was taken.

Another modern-day solution for learning about the individuals appearing in the photograph is the biographical dictionary of the University of N. (1991 edition). It identifies Ernst von Apfeldorf as "a historian specializing in the German Middle Ages."

The two women in the photograph are Frau Kürz, mother of Charlotte Kürz and wife of Heinrich Kürz, and Frau von Apfeldorf, the historian's wife. Both women are blonde. One wears a white blouse under a suit jacket, its neck open wide to reveal a pearl necklace. The other has a flowered dress and a gold cross necklace. Their smiles reveal dazzling teeth and the use of lipstick. Between the table and the bench where the two pipe smokers are seated, a little to the side, is a flag mast, of which the cord can be seen. The flag, if there is one, is outside of the camera's scope. The two men seem to have been interrupted in the middle of a lively conversation. They have raised their eyes towards the camera. Above them hang the shadowy branches of a linden tree, whose trunk cannot be seen. Even the way they both pet the little dog attests to a certain level of closeness between then. The one on the left, closer to the table, is the host of this pleasant gathering: Gustav Tiedemann. He is smiling.

The biographical dictionary describes Gustav Tiedemann as a "college professor of biology" and points out that he directed the dissertation of Emil Schreiber, the famous German-American biologist.

On the map, not far from the marketplace, is a green patch representing Marienfriedhof, a little cemetery that looks more like a public park, with a blue pond. It is marked with the number 3. The tourist center's commentary states that Marienfriedhof contains the tomb of Karl Ludwig Spankerfel, the famous mathematician and physician who died in 1815. Another old tradition dictates that foreign scholars invited to the University of N. be brought to Marienfriedhof to reflect on this tomb.

On the far right of the photograph, the man petting Stefi the dog is the French mathematician Christian Morfaust. The foreign scholar's presence in the little town was probably the pretext for organizing this gathering. Morfaust wears a mask of black leather that hides the majority of his face and ties behind his ears, underneath the sides of his round eyeglasses. Like his friend Tiedemann, he sports a satisfied smile, clearly visible in spite of the pipe.

There is also the Kolloquium register. The huge hardbound register, in which, since 1888, the guests of the Mathematics Kolloquium of Gustav-August University have written summaries of their talks, shows little activity in 1943. Professor Morfaust, from the University of Paris, is the only foreigner to have written in the register since November 4, 1941 (the day Kirill Kristoff, from the University of Sofia, gave a talk on differential equations). Three German mathematicians visited in the meantime. Morfaust used violet ink to write both his name and the title, "On a

Theorem of Spankerfel and Legendre." His summary (originally in French) says:

> We give the formal statement of a theorem on prime numbers, as written by Karl Ludwig Spankerfel in 1809. Adrien-Marie Legendre found a proof for it the following year. We return to this fine example of amicable scientific collaboration.

The talk summarized on the next page of the register dates from 1948.

On the map, number 5 is the N. Museum of Printing. This museum mainly contains engravings and antiquarian books (which are often rare as well). One of the engravings, whose artist is unknown, is reproduced on the map. In spite of the small size of this reproduction, one can recognize a classic character from German legends: a horned, cloven-hoofed demon, with circumflex eyebrows and a pointy beard. He is seated in a public square in front of some gabled houses with his sharp chin resting on his fist and one leg crossed, and he appears to be in conversation with a little dog.

Two people are missing from the photograph: Heinrich Kürz and Frau Tiedemann. The empty chair is probably where the man or woman taking the photograph was sitting. If the photographer was Kürz, the mathematician who invited Morfaust to N., then Frau Tiedemann was busy in her kitchen, and the photo would have been taken without waiting for (or thinking of) her. If it was Frau Tiedemann, then Kürz wasn't there at all, but was rather called back to Berlin or elsewhere by

his military obligations (decoding enemy messages, recruiting collabora-
tors to the German war effort). In front of the empty chair, there is no
drinking glass, which favors the second hypothesis. Nothing allows for
a definite answer, in spite of the inscription on the back.

CHAPTER VII

Trip to N.

(NOTES FROM THE GRAY NOTEBOOK, 2005)

5/1/2005 • On the back of the map of the little town of N., near another photo of the statue on the fountain, the tourist center has included a summary of the town's history, starting 500,000 years ago, lingering over the 17th, 18th, and 19th centuries, and ending with a leap from 1933 to 1945:

> Between 1920 and 1933, the university's reputation grew due to the presence of several renowned physicians and humanists. During World War II, the town escaped the bombings. In 1945, the university reopened. Today, the population is 130,000 inhabitants, of which 20,000 are students.

5/1/2005 **UNIVERSITY OF N.**
ADMINISTRATIVE ARCHIVES

• Photos of Christian M. at the ceremony for the 250th anniversary of Gustav-August University in 1937.

Photo No. 1: His speech in the grand hall, which has been decorated with flags.

Photo No. 2: The French delegation poses in the public square, in front of the gabled houses and the Nazi banners, with a man in a dark uniform (knickerbockers and riding boots, armband) holding a panel for the photographer that reads "Frankreich"; the two men in the delegation are both in French academic dress, one with a handsome mustache, wearing an *épitoge* with three ermine stripes, and M., with his black mask and the Commander's cross of the Légion d'Honneur hanging around his neck over the white cotton *rabat*.

• M. His desire for knowledge (insatiable curiosity) transformed after his injury into a need to be recognized as the best in everything. The physical transformation led to a mental transformation (obviously!). He himself speaks of a "second birth."

5/3/2005 KÜRZ COLLECTION

• Kürz saved everything. His journal (Paris, 1942). Photographs, notebooks, log books, mathematical manuscripts, articles written by others that he annotated, letters he received and copies (carbon) of his own letters. An enormous collection.

5/4/2005 • Correspondence between Kürz and M. No (or very little) math in these letters. Letters twelve pages long. Their common love of Greater Germany. Written in French! A bit boring and then, all of a sudden, a surge of lyricism, to express the love of the French lark, or "alouette," (M.) who flies under the protection of the German eagle (Kürz). The eagle and the lark…

• Other letters, notably from:

- Silberberg, in 1939, from Strasbourg. He sent a lemma.

- Slawek, a Polish mathematician, employed as a feeder of lice (serving as a blood source for lice in order to create a serum to combat typhus). A letter of appeal for help (1943). No carbon copy of a response.

- Ernst von Apfeldorf, thanking him for a dinner invitation, 1950.

- Yersin (senior), Paris, 1942, thanking him for food tickets.

• In Kürz's archives, articles by Silberberg, but also separate copies of his two notes published by the Academy of Sciences. Lots of annotations and writing crossed out in pencil. He really worked on these papers!

→ Must go see the archives of Harold Smith, in Oxford: he worked with Kürz's son-in-law after the war.

5/5/2005   **TIEDEMANN COLLECTION**

• Letters, photos. He lived on Humboldtstrasse.

He was a cellist. His wife, a pianist. Lots of chamber music. A trio with Schreiber, a student of Tiedemann's who played violin.

A photograph shows them in action. The violinist's bright blue eyes. Became a more famous biologist than his mentor. Emigrated in 1938 (his stepfather was Jewish). Found a job at a small university in the American Midwest.

• Another photograph: an evening in his garden on Humboldt Street, in 1943.

This picture leads to a few questions.

> - In 1943, no one could have known that the little town of N. would be spared from the bombings. The threat must have made dinner invitations and receptions risky. Even in pretty houses with gardens, festive gatherings must have been rare.
>
> - What products were available to make a tart, for example? Butter, etc.? What if you were an individual (Frau Tiedemann)? A pastry shop (Korb & Schlag)?
>
> - Who is the doctor in the photo? Haven't found any mention of this Friedrich elsewhere, in any of the university archives. Was he there as a doctor? Called to come treat one of the guests? M.'s neuralgia?

• M.'s presence in the photo, his presence in N., raises more questions.

> - Official forms to fill out in order to enter Germany in 1943, both before traveling and at the border: the usual bureaucratic details, but also a declaration of religion, certifying that one was not Jewish (for French citizens, this was noted on passports).

• Coincidences: the young and brilliant mathematician Otto Zach was reported missing from the Eastern Front (battle of Kursk) the very day M. gave his talk in N.

5/6/2005   On the train (back to Paris), questions:

• Concerning another one of the people present in the photo of the charming summer evening in 1943, Ernst von Apfeldorf. This fact doesn't appear in the university's biographical dictionary, but he was among those addressed in the letter of appeal that Marcel Schmitt sent to several German historians asking them to intervene in favor of Daniel Roth, a historian who specialized in the historical events referenced in Dante's *Inferno*. Evacuated to Clermont-Ferrand with the University of Strasbourg, he was arrested in June 1943 as a member of the Resistance and sent to Germany. He was beheaded in Wölfersheim on December 5, 1943. Impossible to know whether the letters Schmitt wrote actually reached their destinations. Ernst von Apfeldorf, who was well placed and very influential, didn't come forward, according to Schmitt.

• Also in summer 1943: the bombing of Hamburg. 40,000 civilian deaths? Flames 8,000 meters high? Corresponding exactly with the dates of Kürz's visit to Paris (June 1942): the filming of *Les visiteurs du soir* in Paris. The flames coming up to lick the hands of Jules Berry (the devil). How high? A girl's love being stronger than the devil (this is a film!).

• "History is the science of man's misfortunes" (Queneau, *Une histoire modèle*). Mathematical modelling? A truly complex predator-prey system—certain sardines can become sharks, for example.

• Testimonials from those who survived the Nazi camps. During the transportation in uncovered freight cars following the evacuation of Auschwitz (march of death), survivors saw the corners of these cars as relative shelters.

• A circle has no corners. Neither does a cylinder. Hence, perhaps, the descriptions of hell: circles (Dante), a cylinder (Beckett's little book *The Lost Ones*).

• List of hells: Homer (steersmen, the dog of hell), Christian (pain and a black pit), Dante (wretched hearts), Brueghel (succubus, lemures), Goethe (cloven-hoofed demon).

Plus musicians, Liszt (*After a Reading of Dante: Fantasia quasi Sonata*).

And now.

Beckett.

• Thinking of other books. For example: *Painting at Dora* (Dora was the camp where they developed the V-2 rockets). Le Lionnais was deported to Dora. During the roll call, he mentally recreates a museum of paintings (Brueghel at Dora). Painting numbers, which he speaks about with another deportee, beautiful numbers, π, the square root of 2. The finer points of number theory. His book *Les nombres remarquables*, dedicated "to my lifelong friends, delicious and terrifying, numbers." Terrifying? Why terrifying? See, for example, what he says on the 7th positive integer. Or on the 24th?

CHAPTER VIII

One Hundred Twenty-One Days

On the 24th of August, 1944 at 8:45 p.m., the first tanks of General Leclerc's 2nd Armored Division made their entry into Paris via the Porte d'Orléans. The uprising had started on the 13th, the French flag was fluttering over the Sorbonne on the 19th, the Hôtel de Ville and the ministers were free on the 20th, but the fighting wasn't over and Paris was covered in six hundred barricades. On August 25th, at the Montparnasse train station, Colonel Rol-Tanguy and General Leclerc accepted the surrender of the German troops. The most beautiful day of our lives, some said. That's it, it's over! We're going to live again! everyone thought. The black vehicles were covered in a rainbow of summer dresses and flags. People were singing "La Marseillaise," girls were dancing in the streets and boys were kissing them.

This glorious and symbolic liberation was soon joined by the liberation of Troyes, in the east, and those of several cities in the Paris Basin and the middle of France.

On August 27th, Clermont-Ferrand was liberated as well. This, too, was a collective outpouring of jubilation. The female Alsatian students who had been taking refuge in the town along with the University of Strasbourg for almost five years made traditional costumes with big black headdresses and danced in the Place de Jaude.

It's over, thought Mireille and her mother, we can go back home.

Since the end of June 1942, the two women, both Parisians, had been living (or, in any case, surviving) in a hamlet near the town, more or less hidden away with the villagers' discreet complicity. The two of them had left Paris and crossed the Demarcation Line a few days after it had become mandatory to wear the star, just before the big roundups in July. Only Mireille and her mother were mentioned in the previous sentences because Mireille's father died "*pour la France*" during the fighting that took place in May 1940. As for the star, it came up because French law had decided that Mireille's mother Nicole, with a maiden name of Gorenstein, was Jewish, and therefore so was Mireille. This imposed Jewishness was a novelty for the two women. It did not accompany any religious beliefs, any rituals, any family traditions—in fact, not one specific thing Nicole and Mireille could have possibly shared with other "Jews" or "half-Jews." What's more, the women had thought for a few weeks afterwards that because Mireille's father, a Parisian lawyer from a family of practicing Catholics (though he himself was an atheist and a free thinker), had been killed in action, they would be protected from the anti-Semitic decrees of October 1940. They had quickly understood that that wouldn't be the case. But now it was over, France was going to be free, they were going to live again.

In September, when there was fighting around Metz (because the war wasn't actually over), Mireille and her mother arrived in Paris, the same day the leaders of what had been previously known as the French State were taking refuge in Sigmaringen, Germany.

On Rue de Médicis, the women's apartment had been emptied of all its furniture. They found the dining room table and chairs with a neighbor, who had kept them in expectation of the women's return (so she said). But they would never know what became of the rosewood desk and bookcase from the law office, or the bathtub. The fact that all the books had disappeared upset them more than the loss of their armchairs, beds, linens, or dishes. Living again… Yes. To start, one had to find mattresses to sleep on. Eating again… not quite yet. So much energy was needed to procure something to eat. Something to cover up with, as well, because autumn, cool and wet, had arrived. So much time was lost in the displacements. The price of a bicycle was unimaginable. Fortunately, certain sections of the metro were starting to work again, when there was electricity.

It was over. People were reconnecting, writing to friends with whom they'd been out of touch, for years in most cases. Some wrote back, others didn't. People were visiting each other. Information was spreading. Letters arrived from a cousin who was being detained as a prisoner of war. One of Mireille's neighbors and classmates was beaten and her head was shaved in public, all because someone claimed to have seen her walking with a German soldier in the Jardin du Luxembourg. One of Nicole's cousins, a brilliant young professor and the head of a Resistance network, had been denounced as a Jew by a fellow Frenchman and hanged. Another was said to have been killed along with his wife by the French Militia; both were supposedly found later with insulting words written on their bodies. Yet another had been shot for acts of resistance. Or deported to Germany.

But of the ones sent there, there was almost no information.

Since the women's return, Mireille's mother had received news of her brother Robert, who was confined to the Saint-Maurice psychiatric hospital, and with whom she had not been able to communicate for several years. Like the other patients, he had mainly suffered from the lack of food during the occupation, but he had really made the best of the situation, having even managed to publish mathematics articles under a pseudonym that he had abandoned as soon as the liberation of Paris was announced—proof that he had continued to be interested in current events. That's what the psychiatrist, a Doctor Busoni, wrote to Nicole in his response to her letter. She went, a little on the metro and a lot on foot, to the hospital, which she hadn't done since Mireille was born.

"The worst is behind us," the doctor said to her.

"I'm fine," Robert said to her.

And when she was concerned to find him thinner:

"Well, you're thinner, too," he observed.

She told him, in a few minutes, about her two years of life with Mireille in Clermont-Ferrand. He also had news for her.

"Doctor Meyerbeer was seized in a roundup of Jews, taken to Drancy, then deported to a camp in eastern Germany, or maybe Poland," he explained to his sister. "But it's over, the war's going to end," he, too, added. "And he's going to come back," he said. "Or maybe not."

In October, it rained almost every day. Mireille's mother went back to her job teaching high school at the Lycée Chaptal. On the first day, an actor read a Resistance poem called "The Night

Watchman of Pont-au-Change" during the tribute to the former students who had been killed by the Germans. Its author, Robert Desnos, was still in captivity somewhere. The bugle calls, the minutes of silence, and the memorial wreaths marked the start to the new school year.

In the Jardin du Luxembourg, which Mireille could see through her bedroom window, the wet paths were covered in dead leaves. Torrents of water fell on the day the news came that Athens had been liberated. And then, a week later, the Allies entered Aix-la-Chapelle, finally, a German city, the first one. Like everyone else, Mireille and her mother were listening to the news on the radio and the remarks people made while waiting in line to buy food. And like everyone else, they were moving around little flags on maps of Europe. A mass of happiness and hope had irrupted in August, from which no one could completely escape.

On November 11th, Churchill and de Gaulle walked down the Champs-Élysées together, to the cheering of an innumerable crowd. Mireille and her mother were there, too, with some rediscovered friends. And it was the first day of classes at the universities. At Clermont-Ferrand, Mireille had started studying German literature. When she enrolled in classes at the Sorbonne, she added Dante and Petrarch to Goethe, Schiller, and Heine. The professors, at least all those who were in Paris, returned to teaching. Many among them had just been reinstated to their teaching positions after being previously dismissed by Vichy. Several had been detained in stalags or oflags, others had been arrested, some had even been shot while working for the Resistance. Two or three collaborators had been subjected to the purge, but in a quite merciful way—a few weeks of suspension that were already over. Some had been sentenced to prison, but they would be out soon. To have possibly loved a German was more objectionable than having definitely loved the Greater German Reich. And besides, for its reconstruction, France needed all the help it could get.

At the end of November, the news finally came that the 2nd Armored Division had liberated Strasbourg. Two days later, in Paris, during the formal ceremony marking the beginning of the new academic year at the Sorbonne, Mireille heard a reading of the "Song of the University of Strasbourg," a poem Aragon had written the previous year. But the professors and students from Strasbourg who had been arrested were still being held in Germany. It's over, the Silberbergs are going to come home, thought Mireille as she moved one of her little flags, I'm going to write to Clara. But she didn't.

In December, the German army regained the offensive in the Ardennes. On the map, the space occupied by Nazi flags wasn't shrinking very much. Maybe it wasn't really over. After the dead leaves, after the rain, Mireille spent hours watching the snow fall from the top of her windows onto the deserted paths of the Luxembourg gardens. The fog was freezing onto the windowpanes. She would examine the delicate forms of the tiny frost crystals, trying to imagine what André would have said if he had been there to look at them with her. She would remember the words he had used to talk about numbers, his jokes about the inverse powers of 2, like $1/2$, $1/4$, $1/16$ Jewish blood: "Ah, you're only half Jewish, 1/2 for you, 3/4 for me, that would make 5/8 for our children, and a great fractions exercise!" He would say words like "symmetry" and "star," we would laugh together about a delicate six-pointed star composed of solid water frozen on a window. But André wasn't there. Where had they taken him? she wondered as she scrutinized the map.

When January began, it had already been snowing for two weeks. People celebrated the new year as best as they could. It would be the year of victory and, in expecting victory, everyone could tighten their belts a little more. Once again, Strasbourg was under threat. But after the blue, white, and red flags of the Allies finally signaled the defeat of the Germans in the Ardennes, then in Strasbourg, other little red flags far to the east responded: the Russian army entered Warsaw.

Seated in the middle of the crowd of students gathered in the seats of the big lecture hall, Mireille attended another ceremony, over which de Gaulle himself presided, that officially marked the liberation of the university. It was so cold in Paris that Mireille spent whole days in January in her coat and gloves working underground in the metro, where the temperature was more tolerable than in the university library. The winter was even worse in the east, according to the newspapers, which were being printed on a single sheet because of the paper shortage.

The little red flags cleared the Oder on January 31st, then, on February 14th, the blue, white, and red flags of the Allies crossed the Rhine. Snippets of unbelievable information started to arrive about the camps the Red Army had liberated in Poland. The war was soon finished, German cities were being bombed, Dresden had been reduced to ashes, and, at the beginning of March, the Allies' flags arrived in Cologne. Finally, a big city, a symbol. Standing at her window, Mireille watched the park's bare trees while thinking about the big gothic dome reflected in the Rhine, an image from one of Heine's poems. Two years already, she realized. It was on the 23rd of February, 1943, that she had first seen André.

In March, Mireille went back to Strasbourg for the first time. It was, she would think to herself even long afterwards, the coldest day of her entire life. The harsh winter wasn't over yet. She had left the train station and asked for directions; she remembered the name of the street, since André had told her about his parents' shop and she remembered every word he had said to her. It wasn't too far. She entered the Silberberg's store, with the book she wanted to return to them, which was wrapped in an old newspaper, clasped tightly to her chest.

"*Bonjour*, Madame," she had said. "Do you remember me? I'm one of André's friends."

"Not at all," André's mother replied after having looked her up and down. "We don't know you."

And because Mireille was about to protest, give her name, explain herself:

"This is a store, we have work to do. Go away!"

And she had turned her back on Mireille. Out on the street, the wind stung her like another slap in the face. Of course she recognized me. At Clermont, André had asked Clara to invite

Mireille over to their house. Clara hadn't been very happy about it, but she had done it anyway, she always did what her brother asked her, and she had introduced Mireille to her parents—that was in April of '43, two months before André had been arrested. And now his mother was refusing to speak to her. But why? That's what they call rejection. She would not be hearing anything from André's parents. Mireille took a train back home, put the *Inferno* in her bag—the book with the dedication to André and Daniel Roth's signature inside. Back in Paris, she wrote to Clara, who had been her friend, and with whom she had taken Professor Schmitt's course at Clermont-Ferrand on the Alsatian humanists. Clara didn't write back.

In April 1945, everyone knew it really was the end this time. The little flags finished covering the map of Europe, with red ones around Berlin, then, on April 24th, red ones in Berlin. It was over. Vichy France was declared null and void, the head of the so-called "French State" arrived in Vallorbe, on the Swiss border, then was brought back to France, where he would be put on trial. As for Hitler, he wouldn't be—he had committed suicide.

What a marvelous month May was! Once more like in one of Heine's poems, all the buds were bursting. The most beautiful day of our lives, everyone kept saying. The war was over. Everyone went to the Champs-Élysées again to watch the military victory parade. They're going to come back, thought Mireille. In the flowering Luxembourg gardens, in front of the old edifice of the Sorbonne, on the Boulevard Saint-Michel, on the banks of the

Seine, people strolled, hummed, smiled at strangers. As she walked down the boulevard on her way to class, Mireille looked at the beautiful books in the windows of the secondhand bookstores. Hardbound law books, some of which might have belonged to her father. Books on mathematics. Stolen from whom? she wondered. The German bookstore on the Left Bank had closed, the florist who had employed Mireille for a few months during the occupation had reopened his kiosk, it was a time to give flowers, and business was good, even without those arrogant Germans who showed up in June 1942.

With the war over, the prisoners of war were starting to arrive at the Gare du Nord station. It was a time not to die, as the poets would say. But the extermination machine was well underway and continuing to kill, even killing poets, even the night watchman of Pont-au-Change, with exhaustion, disease, typhus.

A few of the surviving deportees were also starting to return.

In the month of June, Mireille, who was shy and reserved by nature, but determined nonetheless, went to wait for Henri Pariset at the end of one of his classes. André had told her all about his professor, but since Pariset had been appointed to Paris in 1940, he had already left Clermont when she got there, so she had never met him. She arrived well in advance and waited for a long time in the hallway of an institute on Rue Pierre-Curie. Through the door to the lecture hall came words she didn't understand. From time to time, groups of men having discussions, probably mathematicians, would pass by, looking at her for a moment, then returning to their conversation. The gaze of one of the men—who had a red lock in his graying hair and wore a leather mask, as well as the somber clothes and black armband typical of someone in deep mourning, which didn't keep him from laughing very hard—frightened her. Only a woman with a typewriter in her arms stopped to ask Mireille if she needed any help. She was the one who pointed out the hidden door where the professor would come out. Finally, there was the sound of commotion, seats slamming back up: the class was over. Pariset came out, with a little chalk on his nose and a lot on his sleeves. She approached him, introduced herself, and said she was a friend of André Silberberg's. He took the sad girl to a café on Rue Saint-Jacques, listened to what she had to say, guessed without much effort what she wasn't saying, confirmed that André had been sent to a camp in Upper Silesia, was a little surprised that she didn't know that already, since the Silberberg family had been informed, but didn't comment on it. He said that he had written letters to André and that the first letter he had received was a piece of paper André had thrown off the train as it was leaving Drancy. Mireille lowered her eyes to her glass of grenadine and he saw by this that she had received one, too.

"He had signed it as André Danglars," he added. "That was the pseudonym he used to publish his last two mathematics articles."

He had signed as André, thought Mireille, and she smiled as she remembered how André had laughed in explaining his choice of pseudonym to her. Pariset had then received a postcard from André, written in German and signed with his own name, sent from the camp. Pariset had rushed him a package, for which André had acknowledged receipt with a second postcard. Pariset explained the mechanism of this correspondence: the card would arrive in the offices of the *Union Générale des Israélites en France* (the Union of Jews in France), an office created by Vichy France, he clarified, but Mireille knew what the UGIF was. But she didn't know about how this correspondence worked, which is what Pariset explained to her. The UGIF would call in the addressee and give him or her the letter, along with an official memo stating the rules that had to be followed when writing a response. Pariset had thus written back (in German). He specified that the first postcard from André had taken more than six months to get to him, that André had said in it that he was doing well, he was keeping his spirits up, and he had asked that the professor pass this news along to his family and friends. Pariset added that the card had most likely been addressed to him because André didn't want to risk putting anyone in danger, and that he, Pariset, a professor at the Sorbonne and, above all, a non-Jew, was a good recipient. Writing to his family, who were hiding in Clermont-Ferrand, would have been too dangerous. For the same reasons, André hadn't given the names of the friends he was thinking of.

"That's why I wasn't able to let you know," Pariset added kindly.

But Clara could have, thought Mireille. Pariset then said he was already working on getting a scholarship for André so that he could start working on his dissertation again as soon as he returned.

"Without a doubt," he concluded, "a tall, handsome, athletic boy like André has made it through. He's going to come back."

The mass of hope took shape once more. He was going to come back. It had already been two years since the roundup in Clermont. Mireille looked at the flags on the map of Europe—Upper Silesia had been liberated in January. They now knew that the camp, which was called Auschwitz, had been evacuated of almost all its deportees before the Red Army had arrived. So where would he be coming back from? And when? The surrender hadn't taken place until May 8th, they would have had to find trains for them, of course, and then how many days would it take to come back from so far, because it was far, across a devastated Germany, on railways that had suffered so many bombings? Maybe he got sick, they had treated him, that had caused the delay. He wouldn't be delayed any longer, others were already coming back. She went to the Hotel Lutetia, where they were taking in the survivors, in the joy of some, but in the anguish and pain of all. She came home terrified. And what about him, what had become of him?

They were coming back. In July, Pariset wrote Mireille to say that Doctor Sonntag, a friend of the Pariset family who had been at Auschwitz with André, had returned to Strasbourg. He had arrived from Buchenwald in April, but had left almost immediately to go help deportees returning from Bergen-Belsen. Now that he was back, he was gradually starting to see patients again. The mass of hope was unraveling. Mireille called, arranged an appointment, caught a train, walked through Strasbourg while avoiding the Silberberg's shop, sat patiently in the waiting room, and was finally called in by the doctor, to whom she admitted that she wasn't sick, but rather that she was a friend of André Silberberg's and Professor Pariset had told her that, just maybe, the doctor would be able to give her news about André.

"My friend Pariset called me. He told me about you," said

Sonntag, taking her by the shoulders.

He led her to the end of the hallway into the living room of his apartment, entrusted her to his wife, finished his appointments.

"Now," he said upon returning, "we have time to talk."

He told Mireille that he had seen André every day for a year and a half, that they had spoken a lot, that André, as always, wouldn't go down without a fight.

"Did you know that before the war, I had to give him stitches after a brawl?"

Mireille remembered the discretion and pain with which André had told her about his life in Strasbourg and his rebellions before the war.

"He told me he'd had to have stitches, but I didn't know that was you."

Sonntag told her about how he and André had been assigned to the Revier, the camp's infirmary, until January, when all three Auschwitz camps were suddenly and violently evacuated. He didn't say anything about the conditions in which they had lived for the eighteen months before, but he did talk about how he and André had walked side by side, in the snow, for forty-eight hours, after which they had arrived alongside a railroad and had been made to climb into uncovered freight cars. There had been a lot of pushing and shoving, during which he and André became separated. He had ended up in Buchenwald. He didn't know where André had been sent.

"One of my colleagues was in the same group as André," he said to Mireille, "Doctor Meyerbeer, a psychiatrist. He got to know André well at the camp. Maybe he'll be able to give you some news.

I'm not sure what became of him. But I know he practiced at the Saint-Maurice Hospital. It should be easy to find out if he's come back, or when he will come back. I wrote to the hospital and no one has answered, not yet anyway, but I should hear something soon. When they have news about him, I'll let you know."

Mireille still had questions. She asked Sonntag if he knew Daniel Roth, the historian André had told her about, who had signed the book by Dante.

"He was my cousin," Sonntag said. "A historian, a great mind, and a member of the Resistance. One of his colleagues, Marcel Schmitt (Mireille recognized the name of the Renaissance specialist whose class she had taken at the Sorbonne), tried to get some German historians to intervene in his favor. With no success. Daniel was beheaded."

There was silence for a moment. He could see her hesitating once more.

"Please don't ask me about that," he stopped her gently. "We did our best to never talk about anything too personal. Adding that kind of pain would have killed us. André and I spoke about mathematics and medicine. He was still thinking about his dissertation; he would give arithmetic and geometry problems to the deportees to help them keep their minds occupied. Have you visited his family?"

"It wasn't a very warm welcome," Mireille answered, and she smiled. "You could even call it icy. To tell the truth, they really didn't want to speak to me," she finally added.

They treated me like a dog, she thought to herself, but didn't say so.

"I know them," the doctor said, "I've been their doctor for years. That's how they deal with suffering. Their anguish is all they have left of their son, and they don't even want to share that."

The Sonntags put her up for the night, then she took a train back. Like in a Romantic poem, it was a radiant summer morning. In the train compartment, people were commenting on the reports from Pétain's trial. She closed her eyes so that she didn't have to join the discussion.

"Meyerbeer, yes," said her mother, "I know him, he's the one who was treating Robert. He was deported. They might have news about him now."

And Nicole returned to Saint-Maurice, where her brother sadly welcomed her. "He's not coming back," he said. Doctor Busoni confirmed it. They had just found out that Doctor Meyerbeer died in January after the Auschwitz camp was evacuated. And they gave her the name and address of the survivor who had brought the news.

His name was Louis Klein and he lived in Paris, near the Raspail metro station. It was through him that Mireille finally found out about André's death. He didn't know André's last name, only his first name: André, his name was André. That was why he hadn't been able to let anyone know. He recognized him in a photograph, taken at Clermont-Ferrand during a picnic, that Mireille showed him.

"That doesn't really look like him," he said, but then he started over.

It wasn't that the photograph didn't look like him, but rather that the deportee he had known in January 1945 didn't look like him.

"That's him, those are his eyes, and he was from Strasbourg, a mathematician, his name was André, no doubt about it. I'm sorry to be the one to tell you," he said, "but he died. Right before my eyes."

And he started to cry.

Not Mireille. She wanted to know, she waited. They had met after the march, on the train; they'd ended up in a corner of a freight car. A corner was a relative shelter—Klein explained how Meyerbeer had fallen, been trampled on, and died, from that or from everything that had come before, and how his body had been thrown off the train.

"Thrown," he repeated, shaking his head. "But André and I," he continued, "after having survived the march, we survived the uncovered freight cars and the snow, and we knew that we were saved, that the war had already ended, that we were going to go home. We were laughing with happiness," he added through tears. "But André died. Two days later, the camp was liberated. It was a makeshift camp, called Mariahilf."

It was over. He hadn't disappeared. Someone had seen him die. Someone knew where he had died. Someone knew what day and what time he had died. It was no longer possible to imagine that he had gotten lost or detained somewhere, in a Saxon forest or a Polish hospital. He wouldn't be coming back. He was dead.

Mireille let the family know, by way of a short letter to Clara. The Silberbergs kept ownership of their grief, which they wouldn't share any more than they had shared their anguish.

She also wrote to Doctor Sonntag and Professor Pariset.

To Daniel Roth, beheaded in a Bavarian prison (whether or

not any of those German historians who had been asked to help had actually cared about his fate); to Pariset's brother, shot as a member of the Resistance with his philosopher cousin; to Robert Desnos, the poet who died of typhus one month after the war ended; to the anonymous millions especially, who weren't done being counted and who wouldn't be coming back; to Doctor Meyerbeer, who was thrown off a freight car in who even knows what country, André Silberberg must be added.

Mireille was remembering, counting the days, calculating. We knew each other, but what does that mean, to know someone? We saw each other for the first time, even before we had really spoken, Clara introduced us, that was February 23rd, he had come to wait for me after Schmitt's class. He was so tall! Then there was the day he played piano in a room at the university, every once in a while a whole group would come to hear him, and he had asked Clara to invite me, "ask your friend with the blue eyes if she wants to come," that was a Sunday, March 7th, he had played Bach, and then Mozart's Fantasia. And then the picnic, a long trip, almost all the way to Saint-Nectaire, mainly to get some cheese from a farmer, on bikes, our landlord's wife had let me borrow hers, it was still cold but it was the first day of spring. How carefree we were! We still hadn't really spoken, and then, one of the girls, Madeleine Feinstein, who was slightly scatterbrained, said she'd never understood anything in math. Another one of them, Simone Bamberger, said it was stupid, but no one knew why she thought it was stupid. And of course Clara said something, that her brother was a genius. I don't know why, maybe because he

was watching me, but I wanted to add my two cents, that I had
an uncle who was a mathematician, but I didn't know him, I had
never even met him. He reacted immediately, I had to say his
name. Ah! Robert Gorenstein, of course he knew him—well, he
knew his work, he had even written to him once, before the war.
Gorenstein had sent him a letter and one of his articles in return,
thanks to which he had found the answer to his question. That day
was March 21st, he rode his bike back with me right to my house,
that is, where Mama and I were staying at the time, leaving Clara
and the others to go back without him. And two days later, on
March 23rd, since the class was on Tuesdays, he was there, outside
the lecture hall when I came out, he was waiting for me. Clara
had caught a cold during the picnic, she had stayed home, which
he knew, of course, that was why he had come. We walked side
by side down the street. Then we saw each other more, we took
walks together, usually without saying anything. And then there
was the time Clara invited me over to their house, that was the
day he gave me his article, "On a Few Theorems from Class Field
Theory," by André Danglars, that's me, he had said while laughing,
that way I no longer risk having my articles rejected.

And April 28th, the day he said it to me.

Mireille always thought "he said it to me," without anything
more, because what he had said was unheard of, in the proper
sense, and also too intimate for her to express with words, even
with the words he had in fact uttered, and which, of course, she
kept hearing.

A few weeks of meetings, of confessions, of happiness, of being
carefree, until the last day they had agreed to meet, June 25th,

when he didn't come. And that was it.

Mireille was counting the days, but how? From February 23rd to June 24th, one hundred twenty-one days, from when, say, our eyes met for the first time. Or from April 28th to June 24th, not even two months. Mireille was counting the days, and the words André had said to her.

Hard words, for life in Strasbourg.

Sad words, for the war, when she had told him that her father had been killed. Before France signed the Armistice with Germany in 1940, André had fought as an aviator, and he had made a friend from Paris, also a mathematician and an aviator, who was killed in flight—that blitzkrieg had been so bloody—he'd had a young wife, they'd been expecting a baby, and then André had added that his friend's father had also been killed, in August 1914, before his son was even born—Mireille had heard the sob in André's voice.

Serious words, to talk about Mozart's Fantasia.

Rebellious words, to tell her about the last class he taught, at the high school in Digne, in December 1940, when his teaching position was revoked in accordance with the Statute on Jews, and about one student, just one, but one student all the same, who had come to shake his hand at the end of the class period.

Joyful words, when he had finished proving his "fundamental" lemma, which had given him so much trouble, this will be in my dissertation, and it'll rile up—Mireille remembered he had said rile up—an arrogant German I know. That's when he had talked about Daniel Roth and Dante's *Inferno*.

Playful words, to explain how he chose his pseudonym. For Silberberg, he could have chosen something related to the French words for "silver" and "mount," like Largent, or Mondargent, but that was too transparent, too risky. He had also thought about Winckler, which was the maiden name of one of his grandmothers who wasn't Jewish, but, alas, it was still a Jewish name, no luck, how he had laughed! So he had translated: Winkel = angle, Winckler = Dangle, Danglars, a real name, a well-known name, and even the name of the traitor in a famous French novel.

Confident words, to say I'm totally safe because I'm publishing under the name of Danglars.

Beautiful words, to describe the numbers he was studying, she had loved the irrational, the complex, the transcendental…

And impassioned words, sweet words, words of happiness.

She had so few of his words left. The words in the letter—a makeshift note, thrown at random to the will of the wind that would carry it far away from the tracks, away from the rain that would not destroy it, to the discretion or indiscretion of the person, a more or less considerate passerby, who would find it—friendly words, of course, but cautious words, so cautious that sometimes in rereading them, she doubted whether there had really been more passionate ones.

She had so few of his words left. She also had a couple of photographs, the note thrown from the train, a mathematics article, and the book he had let her borrow, which she hadn't been able to return to the family. Almost all of the young, carefree people in the photograph from the picnic were dead: that scatterbrain Madeleine, Simone, and André, André who had said, "I'm totally safe because I'm publishing under the name of Danglars." So few saved, so many drowned. A verse from André's Dante came back to her as she looked at this photograph:

And thus the Yawning Deep forever o'er us closed.

in dodecasyllabic verse—even though the original Italian verses of the *Divine Comedy* all have eleven syllables. She had looked in the Sorbonne library for other translations of the end of Canto XXVI,

Until the sea above us closed again.

Hell and the sea, the meter of the poetry, the words and the numbers…

CHAPTER IX

The Numbers

The numbers, in order, starting with the negatives:

-25,   the temperature (in degrees Celsius) in Upper Silesia in January 1945 during the evacuation of Auschwitz

0.577215…,   Euler's constant

0.625   or 5/8 Jewish would have been each of Mireille's and André's children

1   single bullet managed to remove one of M.'s eyes, his nose, and half of his jaw

1.414213…,   the square root of 2, the length of the diagonal of a square with a side of 1

2   grenadiers returning to France in a poem by Heine

3   croissants for a breakfast at the Hotel Raphael

3.14159…, π, the constant allowing one to calculate the length and surface area of all circles

5   daughters (and one son) had Christian and Marguerite M.

6TH   Artillery Regiment, the one in which Gorenstein was serving when he had the sense knocked out of him

7   kilometers, the distance between Monowitz and the main camp of Auschwitz

8   minutes, the length of time it took for Sacco to die on the electric chair

9   Rue de Médicis, the home of the Duvivier family

11,   answered the nurse when the numeromaniac polytechnician asked her for a number

12,   the number of syllables in a translation of one of Dante's hendecasyllabic verses

12.3569111418…,   Gorenstein's constant

13TH   of August, the date the uprising started in Paris in 1944

14   years old, Claude Yersin's age when he was looking for his uncle's remains on the battlefield

14.134725…,   the imaginary part of one of the zeros in the zeta function

15   years old was the boy when they decided to send him to Paris

16   meters, the height of the cylinder Beckett describes in *The Lost Ones*

17   years old, Kürz's age when he enlisted in the navy

18TH   of January, the day the Auschwitz camps were evacuated

19   years old, the age of the future great poet when he jumped out of a trench

20   years that Meyerbeer studied Gorenstein

22   years old, Gorenstein's age when he committed a triple murder

23RD   of June, the date Christian and Marguerite were married

24TH   of June, the last day Andre and Mireille saw each other

25   the only square that becomes a cube when you add 2 to it

26, the canto number in the *Inferno* in which the sea closes over Ulysses and his companions

27 German physicists were winners of the Nobel Prize of Physics

28 is a perfect number

29 days had the month of February in 1916

31 years old, André's age when he died in Mariahilf

39, the number of survivors from the convoy in which Silberberg was taken

40 prisoners were held in each cell of the Cherche-Midi prison

41, the largest dimension for which Kürz managed to demonstrate Silberberg's lemma

42.8 meters cubed of rubble per person after the bombing of Dresden

48 hours that André and Sonntag marched side by side

50 meters, the circumference of the cylinder Beckett describes in *The Lost Ones*

60, the number of the convoy that took André to Upper Silesia

65, the smallest integer whose square can be written in two ways as the sum of two squares

67 kilometers, the length of what became known as the Auschwitz death march

70 kilos, the weight of the bags of phenyl-beta that Klein had to carry while he was at the camp

80 victories (at least) had been achieved by Guynemer

103   years old, M.'s age when he died

120   pages of M.'s dissertation were recopied by Marguerite

121   days of happiness for André and Mireille

131   cities were attacked by the Royal Air Force

209,   the number of the hospital where Gorenstein's aunt worked as a nurse

250   years old was the University of N. in 1937

340   men in Convoy 60 were sent to Monowitz

400   individual detached houses could have been constructed for the cost of one insane asylum

475,   the number of Mozart's Fantasia in the Köchel catalog

479   is a prime number and one quarter of 1916

491   men and women from Convoy 60 were taken by SS officers and dogs and immediately gassed

600   barricades were erected during the Parisian uprising

800   meters, the track event in which André was university champion

1000,   the number of Jews in the convoys

1796,   the year Bonaparte made his entry into Milan at the head of his young army

1800   meters, the total length of the cylinders in which the V-2 rockets were constructed at Dora

1801,   the year Beethoven composed his fourteenth sonata *Quasi una fantasia*

1821,   the date Heinrich Heine evoked the books burned during the Reconquista

1858,   the opening of the Kaffeehaus & Konditorei Korb & Schlag in N.

1926,   the year Vito Volterra invented a model for predator-prey systems

1933,   the date the books of Heinrich Heine were joyously burned in public squares

1949,   Gorenstein's death

1950,   the lovely summer evenings were started again in N.

2066,   the year M.'s writings will enter the public domain

8000   meters high, they say, was the height the smoke reached after the bombing of Hamburg

14521.8   square kilometers of Germany were allocated to France by the Versailler Diktat

116800   Reichsmarks would have been the cost of a mentally ill patient if he had been looked after for forty years

157034,   the number tattooed on a survivor's arm and jotted down on a page from a blue notebook

CHAPTER X

The Binder

From a blue notebook, torn pages: notes from another visit to N., notes on Kürz and M. from the information given and the archives lent by Pierre Meyer, with various documents attached… all rearranged in chronological order and divided into eighteen pouches in a red binder.

POUCH 1
NOTES ON PIERRE MEYER

Met for the first time in September 2006. Born January 13, 1915. M.'s son-in-law and Silberberg's friend. A great eyewitness. Several interviews recorded in November and December 2006.

Summary: born and raised in Strasbourg, studied mathematics, worked at the library before the war. Friend of Silberberg, involved in anti-Nazi resistance groups. Mobilized (in an anti-aircraft defense unit, near Nevers). After the Armistice with Germany, demobilized, decides not to return to Strasbourg: Alsace, annexed by the Reich, is too dangerous for him, with his name listed and put on file for his political actions (his father was Jewish, even though he was killed in the German uniform in 1915). In Paris, false papers, works in the offices of the French national railway (SNCF) under a false identity. Transportation of leaflets and more, for a Resistance network, on bicycle or on foot. Takes part in the fighting for the liberation of Paris. Wounded in the arm, he cannot rejoin the army. Stays in Paris and goes back to studying mathematics, after five years' interruption. Classes with Pariset and M. at the Sorbonne. Through Pariset, meets Mireille Duvivier. By chance, also meets Bernadette, a medical student and his future wife. Coincidentally, she is M.'s daughter.

Coincidences… the publication of M.'s letters in the planning stage in 2005, return to N. in 2006. While seeking out the beneficiaries, met Pierre Meyer. He saved Bernadette M.'s papers, among which was the diary kept by her mother, Marguerite Janvier, during World War I, along with letters, announcements. And Mireille Duvivier's papers. Thanks to Marguerite's diary from the hospital, connection with Gorenstein. From Pierre, information on Silberberg and the story of Mireille Duvivier (another connection with Gorenstein) and her one hundred twenty-one days of happiness.

POUCH 2
HANDWRITTEN LETTER FROM IGNACE M.
TO HIS SISTER BERNADETTE (10-15-44)

(copy, original with Pierre Meyer)

Paris, October 15, 1944

My dearest big sister,

Since you left for Normandy two weeks ago, things have gotten worse here. I know you're looking for peace and solitude in the country, but I'm writing to ask you to please return to Chatou because Mama is not at all well. She is very depressed, does not talk to anyone, and spends all day in a chair or in bed, staring into space, doing nothing. I don't know what has caused this listlessness. Maybe it's simply the repercussions of the strange and terrible years we've just lived through.

You and I have already spoken about this, and I still don't know what she really thought about Papa's public stances and his German friends. Now with the Liberation, and Papa's suspension, maybe this, too, is eating away at her. Our grandparents' arrival has not helped things. Grand-Papa is very authoritative and, since the time he and Grand-Mama arrived, it feels like he's the one in charge of the house. For several days, because of the state Mama is in, Marthe has been taking care of everything, but under Grand-Papa's orders.

I beg you, my dear Bernadette, please don't show this letter to anyone. I'm sure Papa will take care of things in order to impress the purge committee and nothing will happen to him.

I'm also sure Mama knows this, she's used to it, so on the one hand she has no reason to worry and on the other, it's actually more depressing. I must add that our grandparents didn't need to come all the way here. Grand-Papa screams that Papa is an imbecile, and the atmosphere reminds me of the worst points of Papa's anger when we were little. We're nearly expecting to witness a belt beating, like the time when you secretly brought me chocolate, do you remember? When I see them together, I'm almost sure Papa was beaten with a belt when he was a child, too.

Even though the tense atmosphere I've described here is worse than it was before you left, you have to come back. Mama needs someone who will talk to her like you do, Thérèse has far too much to do taking care of the baby, and the three others can only fall down on their knees and pray. My dear Bernadette, I beg you, come back.

Your little brother who loves you,
Ignace

P.S. What's more, I'm going to need a little support as well: I'm being reprimanded for going to Tiedemann's house in Germany to join the Compulsory Work Service, and I have to explain myself in front of a committee at school. See why you can't stay far away?

Note: Research trip (under the cover of forced labor) for the son, perhaps negotiated over the dinner of July 1943? How could one possibly know?

POUCH 3
WRITTEN NOTES ON M.

M.'s statements at the purge committee (summarized by Pierre Meyer): the sole aim of his relations with the Germans was to ease the plight of our prisoners of war; the talks in Germany had been ordered by the minister.

→ Look in the archives of the purge committee (at the National Archives).

Announcement: It pleased God to call to Himself Marguerite Janvier, wife of M., deceased on the 28th of February, 1945, after a long and painful illness.

→ M.'s wearing of mourning clothes was ostentatious (per Pierre Meyer).

→ M.'s second daughter, Marthe, took care of him (she stopped her studies) from when Marguerite died until her own death in 1990.

→ Pierre and Bernadette were married in December 1945, a civil ceremony (Ignace M. was Bernadette's witness, Mireille Duvivier was Pierre's witness, no announcement?). After completing their studies, she became a pediatrician and he a professor of mathematics. Two daughters, Andrée and Nathalie, born in 1948 and 1950.

→ Does M. have any other surviving archives? Pierre Meyer doesn't know.

POUCH 4
HANDWRITTEN NOTES TAKEN AFTER THE
INTERVIEWS WITH PIERRE MEYER
(Pages torn from the blue notebook)

On Doctor Sonntag. See the booklet dedicated to him by the University of Strasbourg. Evacuated to Clermont in 1939, arrested as a member of the Resistance, sent to Drancy as a Jew, Convoy 57 for Auschwitz. At Monowitz, directs the Revier (sick bay? the word "hospital" hardly seems accurate). He gets Silberberg assigned there (one of his patients from before the war). Meets Meyerbeer (the psychiatrist), who is also deported and treated (?) at the Revier. Buchenwald after the death march (evacuation of Auschwitz). Resumed his life in Strasbourg, testified at Nuremberg, wrote a text, in 1947, on Monowitz marked with an incredible sense of responsibility.

On Silberberg. See the booklet on Sonntag and Louis Klein's book. Mobilized (in aviation) in 1939. After the armistice and demobilization, appointed senior teacher at a high school in Digne, then dismissed (Statute on Jews of October 3, 1940). Then (December 1940? January 1941?) in Clermont-Ferrand (research in number theory, private tutoring to earn a living). Rounded up by the Nazis in June 1943. Drancy, Convoy 60 for Auschwitz. Secretary of the Revier at Monowitz. Died at Mariahilf in April 1945.

POUCH 5
NOTES TAKEN AT THE LIBRARY OF THE
CHEMISTRY LABORATORY IN P. (12-18-08)

(François Ollier Archive Collection)

Huge archives, lots of information on the France-Germany Committee, then the collaboration (great for those who want to write a biography of Ollier!):

- Family letters, newspaper clippings. Military passbook. Notebooks. His wife's scrapbooks (recipes, invitations).

- Carbon copy of a letter, addressee unknown, recounting the reception at Göring's (Olympic Games of 1936), "a whole new world is emerging," five typed pages.

- Newsletter from the France-Germany Committee, 1937.

- Letter to the weekly magazine *Les Temps Nouveaux*, 1941.

- Letter to the chemists of IG Farben, 4-6-43.

- Incarcerated until 12-23-44 at Les Tourelles camp. Freed (under surveillance).

- Notes for the lawyer: "Relations with German authorities in order to defend the freedom and maintenance of the scientific press. I have never had any contact with students, and I cannot be reprimanded for having exerted any kind of harmful influence on young people."

- Notes "for an appeal from my colleagues to the judge": "I was added to the Groupe Collaboration by surprise, resigning from it would have been viewed as tactless."

- Petition to the Minister of the Interior.

- Case closed, March 1948.

POUCH 6
LETTER FROM HENRI PARISET
TO MIREILLE DUVIVIER (3-19-48)
AND LETTER FROM SAMUEL REISKY
TO PARISET (3-10-48)

(Copies, the originals belong to Pierre Meyer)

Paris, March 19, 1948

Dear Mademoiselle,

I hope that you are in good health and that your work at the National Library continues to be enjoyable. I'm forwarding you a letter I have just received from the United States which I'm sure will interest you.

Warmest regards,
Henri Pariset

P.S. You can keep the letter.

★

New York, Wednesday, March 10, 1948

Dear Professor,

I knew André Silberberg at the Monowitz camp. He was very nice. He gave the prisoners German lessons. He explained number theory, he drew a square in the dirt and said "here's the root of 2." I forget now, but he explained "perfect" numbers. Once, he gave a talk on quantum theory. He spoke about you, his professor. He helped us a lot. Excuse my French, it's

not very good, I can't write very much. I was born in a vil-
lage in Poland, but I lived in Paris (Rue de Ménilmontant).
Now I live in the United States and I'm learning English.
Someone told me he's dead. I'm very sorry to hear that.

Kind regards,
Samuel Reisky

How do you talk about Auschwitz?

POUCH 7
ANNOUNCEMENT FROM *LE MONDE*

(Newspaper clipping)

Nicole Duvivier, née Gorenstein,
and her daughter Mireille
are saddened to announce the death,
at the age of 56, of

ROBERT GORENSTEIN

mathematician

X 1911

on the 12TH of October, 1949.
The funeral will take place at the crematorium of
Père-Lachaise Cemetery
on the 17TH of October at half past ten in the morning.
No flowers or wreaths please.

The "x" marks his graduation date from the École Polytechnique.

Pierre Meyer's memories: very intimate service, Nicole, Mireille, Pariset with two colleagues, Pierre.

POUCH 8
TRIP TO OXFORD, MARCH 2009

(Harold Smith Archive Collection)

Wonderful collection of mathematical manuscripts. But also lots of letters to his wife. Both died rather young.

Letter from Harold Smith to Barbara Smith (6-8-50) (re-transcribed from the original English).

(To understand this letter, it's important to know that Charlotte Kürz married Wilhelm Hermann (mathematician, student of Kürz) in 1949.)

June 8, 1950

My dear Barbara,

After yesterday's long and serious letter, I'll try to be more trivial today. This time it won't be the description of a library, statues, or monuments, but a pastry shop. This one is called Korb & Schlag (which means "basket and cream"). I had my breakfast there this morning, on Hermann's recommendation. Truly extraordinary. I will try to bring you a few Schokoladekugeln.

I have to go and give my first talk, I'll continue this letter tonight or tomorrow morning.

It's late, but I'm picking up my pen again to tell you about the evening I've just had at the Hermanns'. I was truly quite honoured by their invitation, even more so because they had also invited several of their friends and colleagues, the biologist Tiede-mann and the historian von Apfeldorf—you know, the specialist in the German Middle Ages—with their wives, as well as Her-mann's wife's parents, namely Heinrich Kürz himself—whose work I've told you about, but whom I had never met in person before—and his wife, Frau Kürz, whose first name I didn't hear.

The Hermanns live in a pretty house on Schillerstrasse. It's not very far from the centre of town, in an utterly charming residential neighbourhood. To start, we had pre-dinner drinks in the garden, under a linden tree, between the rhododendrons and rosebushes in full bloom. The dinner was German, but delicious: a Gruyère salad, a pork roast with cranberry sauce and sautéed potatoes, and an apple tart (brought by the Tie-demanns, if I understood correctly). The wine was French, and I have to tell you, everything was perfect. Then, coffee, kirsch, pipes, and music.

Probably owing to the presence of the distinguished historian, the conversation was mainly about the origins of German folklore and fairy tales, in particular the story of Faust—I should really say stories, because there are a lot of them. It was a bit high-brow, but fascinating. I'll tell you everything I learnt as soon as I get back. We also talked about dogs, I think it was because of a tradition from northern Germany in which the devil is accompanied by a dog.

All this naturally took place in German, and I think I managed quite honourably.

Kürz played a Beethoven sonata for us, Sonata quasi una fantasia, *he announced, it's the one we call* Moonlight. *I'm sure you've already heard me say he's a very good mathematician, so I was very impressed that he was also such a good pianist.*

Von Apfeldorf and his wife drove me back to the hotel. I'm stopping now, because it's quite late and I have to give a second lecture tomorrow. By the way, I haven't even said anything about the one I gave today: it went rather well, even if I may have gone a little too fast. I wrote my summary in a huge register that was started in… 1888! I was awestruck to be writing after so many well-known names. This time I'm really stopping.

With all my love, your
Harold

Note: so many linden trees! What differences were there between a summer evening at Tiedemann's in 1943 and a summer evening at Hermann's in 1950?

POUCH 9
RETURN TO N., JUNE 2006

(Heinrich Kürz Collection)

Letter from the medieval historian Ernst von Apfeldorf to Heinrich Kürz (6-9-50) (re-transcribed and translated from the German).

June 9, 1950

Dear Heinrich,

We had such a pleasant time at your son-in-law's yesterday evening! Despite her youth, Mrs. Hermann is a true lady of the house and a perfect hostess. And what finesse! The dinner was exquisite and Mrs. Tiedemann's tart was also a success, as always; Frau Schlag must ask for her recipe! Even the English guest was charming, once we got used to his accent. But the highlight of the evening was assuredly your exceptional interpretation of Beethoven's sonata. And how right you are in saying that it expresses the true German spirit!

Please send my kindest regards to Mrs. Kürz.

Best wishes,
Apfeldorf

Von Apfeldorf describes the same evening as Smith in his letter (cf. pouch 8).

POUCH 10
ANNOUNCEMENT FROM *LE FIGARO*

(Newspaper clipping)

The Mortfaus, Langlois,
Dubois, Meyer, and Besson families
regret to announce the passing of

CHRISTIAN MORTFAUS

X 1911

Croix de Guerre with one mention
Grand Croix de la Légion d'Honneur
Deceased the 11th of November, 1996, in Paris, 7th arr.,
in his one hundred and fourth year.
Succeeded by his children, grandchildren,
and great-grandchildren.
Pray for his soul
The religious service will take place
on the 18th of November at ten o'clock
at the Cathedral of Saint-Louis des Invalides.
The burial will be at two o'clock
in the vault of the Janvier and Mortfaus families
at Père-Lachaise Cemetery.

Pierre Meyer's memories: Bernadette was sick, Pierre didn't go. Even so, he had saved the newspaper clipping. A sign of careful editing: the 7th arrondissement is home to the Hôtel des Invalides (a miserable room, according to Pierre, but he never saw it). Died coming home from the Armistice Day ceremony at the Arc de Triomphe (where he had been taken in his wheelchair).

POUCH 11
RETURN TO N., JUNE 2006

(Postcards, photographs, and various papers)

POSTCARDS.

1. The tomb of the mathematician Spankerfel, covered with ivy.

2. The picturesque accumulation of hundreds of bikes in all colors in front of the train station.

3. A pond with ducks swimming on it.

4. Advertising card from the Korb & Schlag pastry shop featuring a photograph of a meringue tart, part of which is cut in such a way to show that under the meringue are apples.

RECEIPT.

Korb & Schlag
seit 1858 in N.
Goethestrasse 23

Espresso	2,20
Warmer Apfelstrudel	4,40
Euro	6,60

Wir danken für Ihren Besuch
26.06.06 − 9:56

FOUR PHOTOGRAPHS (PRINTED ON NORMAL PAPER).

1. The sign for the Biergarten Paradies, with black and red letters on a yellow background (meeting with Bernhardt Hermann).

2. The gray cement wall with a little green that ran onto a bronze plaque, its text quite readable in copper letters on the dark background: "Where they have burned books, they will end in burning human beings / Heinrich Heine 1821 / Bücherverbrennung May 10, 1933" (1821 for the quotation, 1933 for the book burnings, and no date for the plaque itself).

3. An elegant house with white frilled curtains and green shutters, along with rhododendron bushes and a pergola in the garden.

4. The little stone girl on the fountain, smiling, with her motionless spinning wheel.

POUCH 12
LIBRARY OF THE INSTITUTE OF
MATHEMATICS, N. (6-27-06)

The Kolloquium register with all the names. Among others, M. on July 6, 1943, Smith on June 8, 1950. Completed in 1961. The tradition continues (in modern registers).

Back to the university archives. Still the same day. A wealth of papers. The little town wasn't bombed. The paper didn't burn. The letters are still here. The eagle and the lark as well.

POUCH 13
MESSAGE FROM THE ARCHIVES CONSERVATOR
(7-19-06), TRANSLATED FROM GERMAN

> *Dear Professor-Doctor,*
> *In response to your request of June 27, you have our authori-*
> *zation, provided that you obtain the authorization of the ben-*
> *eficiaries, to publish the letters of Professors Heinrich Kürz and*
> *Christian Mofraust.*
>
> > *Best regards,*
> > *Doktor H. Raffke*

Following is a list of Kürz's beneficiaries. Bernhardt Hermann, the son of Charlotte Kürz and Wilhelm Hermann (both deceased). Met at N. He gave his permission.

POUCH 14
LIST OF M.'S BENEFICIARIES

THÉRÈSE, deceased, married Guy Langlois (deceased), six sons (Mathieu, Marc, Luc, Jean, Pierre, Paul), no response from any of them (planned? Of course).

MARTHE, deceased, single with no children.

ANNE, deceased, wife to Patrick Dubois (living?), one son (Pierre-Marie): no.

BERNADETTE, deceased, wife of Pierre Meyer, two daughters, Andrée (now Andrée Daniel) and Nathalie Meyer-Lemaire: yes for both (thanks to Nathalie, contact with Pierre Meyer).

MARIE, deceased, wife to Jean Besson, deceased, three daughters (Marie-Claude Besson, Berthe Besson, Christiane Mallet): all three, no (exactly the same wording for all three, the same as Pierre-Marie Dubois—planned).

IGNACE, husband of Françoise Durenberger, two sons (Antoine and Georges): yes for both.

One no is enough for it to be no, so it's no.

POUCH 15
M.: UNORGANIZED NOTES FOR
AN IMPOSSIBLE BIOGRAPHY
(RELEASE AROUND OCTOBER 2006)

Allegiance to Nazi Germany; Berlin talks (and others here or there, like in N.) in 1943; Croix de Guerre with one mention from the army; daughters, five daughters and finally one son; embarrassment felt by the purge committee, before whom he didn't even need to take off his mask; freight cars of deportees that were filled, but without his help; geriatrics among whom his life came to an end after the death of his daughter Marthe; hospitalizations on a regular basis; injury of a terrible, glorious, obvious, unforgettable nature; *Je suis partout* and other newspapers in which he participated, in sickness and in health; kudos, speeches, and homages given by the army, Catholics, politicians, scientists; longevity beyond belief, which was also full of suffering; mask of black leather, which may also have been uncomfortable; neuralgia and neuritis; operation after operation; prizes (academic) obtained for his brilliant work in mathematics; quarantine (metaphorical) after the war by certain mathematicians at foreign conventions; rages into which he flew when he feared he wasn't being treated like the best; salons with the Catholic bourgeoisie and the evenings of poetry in which he participated; treatments of all kinds that were tried on him; university professors who gave him the cold shoulder; victim of daily and seasonal suffering; widowerhood too soon; xenografts; yperite, or mustard gas, of which he was fortunately not a victim; zone of ambiguity, the gray zone.

POUCH 16
PUBLICATION OF KÜRZ'S JOURNAL

- Transcription of an interview with Catherine Billotte-Yersin, December 5, 2008.

Summary: her father and grandfather, after the Great War, the occupation, relationship with M.

- Letter of acceptance from the University of Fribourg Press for Kürz's journal, translated and annotated. Dated March 5, 2009. Publication scheduled for January 2010.

POUCH 17
HANDWRITTEN NOTES

(Page torn from a notebook)

6-18-10. Meeting with Louis Klein, the author of *Testimony of a Deportee* (he's the one who reported Silberberg's death at Mariahilf). Born in 1918. Meeting arranged by Pierre Meyer.

    157034

Separate from the pouches, scribbled on the binder's cardboard cover:

    Pierre, April 25, 2pm, Cimetière Montmartre.

CHAPTER XI

The Form of a City…

(PARIS, APRIL 25, 2013)

CIMETIÈRE MONTMARTRE — AVENUE HECTOR-BERLIOZ. All the names. Massé, Pernissin, Masson, Meyer, Rolland, Ruben, Chaiche, Maccini, Fridman. On the monuments, the plaques, the tombs. Tabet (star of David and cross), Greuze, Meyer, Lew, Chaïa, Léger, Berlioz. Pierre, who has just been buried, is another Meyer. Words were spoken, rose petals were thrown on the coffin. I walk a little back from the group. The conversations have started up again. The two women in black are probably his daughters, Andrée and Nathalie. I talked to Nathalie on the phone a few years ago, but I never met her. She was the one who suggested I go see her father. There aren't that many people. The others walking in front with the two sisters must be Ignace's children; the youngest adults are probably the children, and the two boys, both around age ten, the grandchildren. They seem so solemn… Maybe it's their first time attending a burial. Pierre had told me he had four great-grandchildren, but the other two must be too young. There are certainly some friends here (from the daughters' generation) and perhaps some of his former students from the high school as well. I walk behind them—I don't know anyone. It also happens to be a beautiful spring day here. *Im wunderschönen Monat Mai…* Although it's still April and we're on Avenue Berlioz, Heine's tomb is definitely here.

Stendhal's is on the other side, on Avenue de la Croix. I can't see it, but I know it's there, and I can't help thinking about it, no more than I can help recalling his: "On the 15th of May, 1796, General Bonaparte made his entry into Milan at the head of that young army which had shortly before crossed the Bridge of Lodi and taught the world that after all these centuries Caesar and Alexander had a successor."

AVENUE DUBUISSON. Underneath the bridge of Rue Caulaincourt are the iron columns supporting it, forged in 1888 in the blast furnaces of Montluçon. A joyful flowerbed of red and yellow tulips has been planted on the roundabout.

AVENUE PRINCIPALE. Armies of watering cans await the visitors who have come to look after the graves of their loved ones. I discreetly head for the cemetery gate. I will write a letter to Nathalie Meyer: "I was very fond of your father and I want to thank you for allowing me to get to know him." Pierre taught me a lot. I exit the cemetery.

AVENUE RACHEL. Incredibly calm. Funerary dignity (monumental masonry), bistro, funeral parlor, florist. On the 15th of May, 1796, General Bonaparte made his entry...

BOULEVARD DE CLICHY. In contrast, sound and fury. The Moulin Rouge, red, not dark gray like the last time I saw it in a black and white archival photo showing two German soldiers joking with two blonde women. How did you say "sex toys, 2 euros" in German in 1942? Definitely two soldiers: officers like Kürz probably didn't visit this type of neighborhood. Pierre lived right behind it at that time, in an attic room on Rue Véron, he said. He would've done what he'd had to do, transporting leaflets or other things, in a peaceful manner, because I already imagine him at peace.

RUE BLANCHE. I could take bus 68 home. But I'm going to walk for a little while, I'll take it further along. I walk down Rue Blanche. Blanche, Dante, and then I think of Rue Dante and Rue Lagrange, for their assonance. On the sidewalk, an elderly woman walking in the opposite direction up the slope has stopped to catch her breath. I am again reminded of Pierre, who would always make the trip down and back up his three floors to buy the macaroons he used to offer me with the coffee he'd prepare whenever I arrived. I saw him for the last time in February, I believe. He had just celebrated his ninety-eighth birthday. He was invaluable and precise as an eyewitness. And he was funny. He used to challenge me: "Being the historian that you are...," he would give me tests: for example, I managed to find the source for each of the twenty-two articles he had given me, higgledy-piggledy in a big brown envelope—articles that had been saved, over the years, by Marguerite M., Mireille Duvivier, and Pierre himself... He lived a full life and observed his entire century. I pass the Blanche-Calais bus stop—Rue Blanche is blocked, I'll go just as fast on foot.

SQUARE D'ESTIENNE-D'ORVES. The Resistance member with his fine aristocratic name. He was "the one who believed in heaven" in one of Aragon's poems. That may be why they named this square after him. The Church of the Trinity is certainly ugly, but I still think "Trinité—d'Estienne d'Orves" sounds rather nice. He was a polytechnician, too. There are all sorts of polytechnicians. Like the two boys from the same year, Gorenstein and M. The fact that both fell in love with the same girl is quite a common occurrence. That both were wounded in the war is just as common. What's more original is the fact that both were treated in the same hospital, by the same nurse.

RUE DE CHATEAUDUN. A family visiting from the county asks me how to get to the Galeries Lafayette.

I point them towards RUE DE LA CHAUSSÉE-D'ANTIN. Which I take slowly, in order to stay behind them. There are lots of people and lots of the usual stores, the ones that make all cities look like each other. In any case, this is true on the street level, because above that, it's definitely Paris, with its history and its fractures.

I cross BOULEVARD HAUSSMANN. Fittingly. More and more pedestrians, customers, tourists.

Behind the Opera Garnier, I cross RUE MEYERBEER. Meyerbeer, as in the composer of the opera *Robert le Diable*, not Meyerbeer as in Robert Gorenstein's psychiatrist. Meyerbeer, Doctor Meyerbeer, thrown off a train. On the other side, the Garnier's majestic steps. Pierre told me about a memory that his wife, Bernadette, had shared with him (she hadn't been there herself but she knew about it): Kürz, during one of his trips to Paris, had taken Mortfaus to the opera. During his trip in June 1942, he had said he wanted to do it. Apparently, he fulfilled his wish. Pierre had described for me the look of this "broken face" from the First World War, both proud and embarrassed to be climbing the steps of the Paris Opera arm in arm with a German officer in full uniform—which Pierre hadn't even been there to see. No date, not even a direct testimony. I remember that Pierre said that Bernadette had told him that someone had told her that her father… Not very reliable. Pierre told me that Bernadette had told him that Marguerite had told her that she had had nausea on April 8, 1921, while watching a solar eclipse—that still passes the test, but not the other story…

AVENUE DE L'OPÉRA. I turn the corner and turn back around to look at those famous steps. I know lots of stories like that. Certainly true. Or almost. In America, this is called "common knowledge." Actually, in the United States, and concerning Kürz, a story has long been told about the biologist with blue eyes, Emil Schreiber, the one who played in a trio with the Tiedemanns. Supposedly, Kürz offered to "Aryanize" Schreiber's children (who had just one Jewish grandparent—André Silberberg would have called them "quarter-Jews") so that Schreiber could stay in Germany. I'm no longer thinking about taking the bus and then a 68 (another one) slips right by. There isn't much to see on Avenue de l'Opéra: luxury shoes, banks, jewelry, travel agencies, yes, but not one bookstore left. Only the street signs remain for reading.

RUE DANIELLE-CASANOVA. A member of the Resistance, a communist, killed at Auschwitz in 1943, has her street in this neighborhood where there's probably no one left who knows what she did.

And I stop at RUE DES PYRAMIDES. On the 2nd of July, 1798, General Bonaparte entered Alexandria…

RUE DE ROHAN. The tourist population becomes denser.

I pass the arches of the Louvre and walk along the side of the Museum of Decorative Arts in the JARDIN DES TUILERIES. The city is loaded with history, without speaking of the Paris Commune and the war waged on it by the government in Versailles (and the beautiful, chateau-less Tuileries garden that resulted from it). I inevitably find myself in the grandiose perspective between the two Arcs de Triomphe: the Carrousel arch here and, there, down the Champs-Élysées, the Tomb of the Unknown Soldier. I finally understand why it's here, in this same garden, that in May 1939 M. declared his love of Germany and his vision of France and Germany dominating Europe together to his German guest. Today, there's a lot of noise, the happy shouts of a bunch of kids on top of a statue. It's spring break somewhere, but not in Paris, since my daughter is at school today. The two boys in the cemetery must have had to miss class, or else they live out in the country. There's a lot of dust on the garden paths.

AVENUE DU GÉNÉRAL-LEMONNIER. I read the plaque. This general was one of the heroes from the Indochina War. Still thinking of M., I wonder what he did, said, thought, about decolonization and the colonial wars. He was directly concerned, he whose family owned and operated a plantation in Senegal. Too late to ask Pierre.

I've crossed the quay and now take the PONT ROYAL, on which I stop for a moment to contemplate the sparkling ripples of the Seine. *Im wunderschönen Monat Mai…* Not too far from here is the gilded cupola of the French Institute where, probably, the Academy of Sciences is unshakably carrying on with its work. This city may be steeped in history, but I must confess I don't know whether they threw the Algerian protestors into the Seine from this bridge. There was no more night watchman of the Pont-au-Change on the 17th of October, 1961…

I take the RUE DU BAC in front of me. Where I start off by crossing a 68, going the wrong direction. The stores here are very elegant; I pass galleries, monasteries, pastry shops in a style different from that of Korb & Schlag, but very chic as well.

Here, VALMY has its IMPASSE. I cross it and stop to read the plaque, on 46 Rue de Bac: "Roger Connan, shot by the Germans on August 20, 1944, at the age of 28."

At the intersection, I take BOULEVARD RASPAIL. And I choose to walk on the left side, in the shade, which means I've really given up catching a bus. On the median, the chestnut trees are not yet in bloom. But that can be sung— *"April in Paris, chestnuts in blossom…"* After the German Romantic poet, Americans in Paris. Which evokes the Liberation, Mireille, her endless wait. I didn't know Mireille, she had been dead for several years when Pierre told me about her, told me her story. She worked as a librarian her whole life, with specializations in German and Italian poetry, as well as the literature about the camps, the concentration camps, the extermination camps. And she always lived alone. With lots of generosity, Pierre passed all of her stories on to me. Reading letters that weren't addressed to me, intimate diaries hidden at the bottom of linen dressers, agendas, drafts—that's my job. Opening boxes of archives, my heart pounding in my chest, that, too. And did my heart pound less for Pierre's stories than for those old dusty trophies? I cross the boulevard and, in front of the Bank of France, I read another plaque. At this location, an unknown member of the FFI (French Forces of the Interior) died for France on August 21, 1944. Across the street, the Hotel Lutetia—after housing the headquarters of the Abwehr, a German intelligence service, then after taking in the scant survivors returning from the camps—has long been restored to its original purpose. I cross the street again to read the plaque, which I've already come to read several times and which always mentions joy, anguish, and pain. It's impossible here not to think, once again, of Mireille Duvivier. I keep on walking. I can't imagine Mireille in 1945. The private events, like the one hundred twenty-one days of Mireille and André's story, do they not form a sort of chain that holds the threads together—the very fabric of history? The barking of a dog, to which my mind probably wasn't headed, brutally brings me back to today, April 25, 2013, the day of Pierre Meyer's burial. I'm now in front of the "modern" building of the EHESS, the School for Advanced Studies in the Social Sciences, which replaced the Cherche-Midi prison. I know that Dreyfus was incarcerated there in 1894, and that during the occupation, it was used for all sorts of prisoners and members of the Resistance, with forty per cell. I'm walking in the very city Kürz visited in 1942. The beautiful building now hidden by scaffolding once served as a recruitment center for the Service du Travail Obligatoire (STO), which subjected French workers to forced labor in Nazi Germany. In passing, I see the window of the historic bookstore, but I don't stop. I don't really have the heart to go look at tables of books. I remember the intense nausea that came over me when I unexpectedly discovered a "scientific biography" of Georges C. Collaborators are in vogue at the moment. I saw all kinds of books, books by sons and grandsons, some courageous, others scandalous. And piles of books on Céline, who was also a World War I veteran.

RUE NOTRE-DAME-DES-CHAMPS. The metro. Notre-Dame des Champs, our lady of the fields, pray for us. And Saint Marguerite as well. Marguerite M. was a saint. I've realized that I probably can't comprehend the true nature of the relationship between the Catholic nurse and the broken face, the exchange of pain and sacrifice… and why not love, pure and simple?

CARREFOUR VAVIN. Rodin's statue of Balzac is found here. After Stendhal… I'm getting a literature lesson as well this morning. This is a novel, from end to end. Fiction. But *all is true*, like Balzac said, rightly, at the beginning of *Père Goriot*.

On BOULEVARD MONTPARNASSE. The café terraces that, as in Saint-Germain-des-Prés, were once fashionable, are now full of tourists. The words that can be "as murderous as a gas chamber," as Simone de Beauvoir wrote, maybe in one of these cafés, murderous words, answering terrifying numbers. Multiplying 8 Reichsmarks by 40 years then by 365 days to get 116,800 Reichsmarks has nothing particularly terrifying about it; it's the addition of the words "mentally ill patient" and "cost" that makes the calculation murderous.

RUE DELAMBRE. Because Delambre was an astronomer. Lots of astronomers have streets named after them in this arrondissement. And the Jewish astronomer who was still working at the Observatory when M. talked to Kürz about it in June of 1942? He died at Auschwitz a year later. I must confess that at this exact moment, I can't remember his name. It's a tiny ripple of "the irresistible tide of forgetfulness" that the philosopher Jankélévitch spoke about. That overwhelms everything. Despite the ceremonies filled with grandeur and emotion, with brass bands, military parades, and flags, like the one for M.'s one-hundredth birthday, then, three years later, perhaps without fanfare, for his funeral at the church of Saint-Louis des Invalides, almost eighty years after his marriage at Saint-Philippe-du-Roule. The Croix de Guerre and the Grand

Croix of the Légion d'Honneur, this time on the coffin, official figures, speeches, flags. The Association of the Former Students of the École Polytechnique was present, Pierre told me. Once more, M. was treated better than Gorenstein. It's definitely too late, I'm definitely too close to my place now to get a bus. I keep walking down the boulevard.

Now, opposite the CIMETIÈRE MONTPARNASSE. Cemetery to cemetery, poet to poet… Here rests Robert Desnos, the night watchman of the Pont-au-Change, another Robert le Diable. He died, too, "there where our century's destiny bleeds"… How beautifully put, words again, an exquisite formulation for the unspeakable. I pass the building where Louis Klein lives, the man who told Mireille Duvivier about André Silberberg's death in 1945, he who shared a corner of a freight car with André and who later wrote a dreadful little book, in which he simply described what happened. I had come here to see him, along with Pierre Meyer, whom I had picked up from the other side of Paris. I brought my notebook, like always. He was handsome, cheerful, and courteous. He was ninety-two years old. He showed us the pale blue number on his forearm. A bit stupidly, I wrote this number down. He told me, "Yes, André Silberberg, I remember him, of course. But is he dead?" We caused him to suffer by telling him about André Silberberg's death and the terrible conditions in which it happened. Which we knew from his own mouth, from the book he wrote. He started singing us a song by Schumann,

> *Das Lied ist aus*
> *Auch ich möcht mit dir sterben*

"The song is over / I would also like to die with you." A poem by Heine, once again. Then, interrupting himself: "but what were we talking about? André Silberberg, yes, of course, I remember him very well. But is he still alive?" The irresistible tide of forgetfulness had already overwhelmed him. I closed my notebook, I stopped my recorder, and we stayed there, Pierre and I, talking with him.

I come to the PAVILLON DE LA BARRIÈRE D'ENFER. Where the entrance to the catacombs is located. It's already late, visiting hours are over, the usual line of tourists has dissolved.

I read the plaque at the PLACE DU COLONEL-ROL-TANGUY. And I think about all these plaques, about Roger Connan, about the unknown member of the FFI, about Danielle Casanova, about Pierre and the liberation of Paris, about Mireille and the Hotel Lutetia, about the innumerable names who will never have a story other than that of their disappearance. And about Pierre's great-grandson, about the children who play on the statues in the Tuileries gardens, about my daughter. In front of my house, I punch in the code, another number, I climb the six floors, I open the door. Inside, no one is waiting for me: it's not Wednesday, it's not spring break, and my daughter, my best beloved, is at her mother's. I take off my shoes covered with the dust of the Tuileries paths, I sit down at my table, facing the window and Paris, I make a little space amongst my mess, I push a red binder and some blue and gray notebooks full of notes out of the way, I open a pad of lined paper, and, with "desperate but intermittent protestations of memory," I start to write:

Once upon a time, in a remote region of a faraway land, there lived a little boy.

SUPERNUMERARY CHAPTER

(PARIS-STRASBOURG, 2009-2013)

As one of its characters rightly says, this book is a novel, a work of fiction. Its characters are imaginary. Any resemblance to real persons, living or dead, is purely coincidental or due to the permanence of human behavior.

The names of some of these characters have been taken from (or inspired by) various books, including THE LILY OF THE VALLEY (Honoré de Balzac), A GALLERY PORTRAIT and W OR THE MEMORY OF CHILDHOOD (Georges Perec), THE COUNT OF MONTE CRISTO (Alexandre Dumas), and THE MASTER AND MARGARITA (Mikhail Bulgakov).

The book cites, uses, or evokes a certain number of other works, not always explicitly mentioned, including (in alphabetical order and with the corresponding chapter numbers) AFTER A READING OF DANTE (Franz Liszt) – VII; ALMANSOR (Heinrich Heine) – X; APRIL IN PARIS (Vernon Duke & E.Y. Harburg) – XI; CHANSON DE CRAONNE (Anonymous) – II; CHANSON DE L'UNIVERSITÉ DE STRASBOURG (Aragon) – VIII; COMPLAINTE DE ROBERT-LE-DIABLE (Aragon) – XI; CONVERSATIONS IN EXILE (Bertolt Brecht) – IV; DE L'UNIVERSITÉ AUX CAMPS DE CONCENTRATION – TÉMOIGNAGES STRASBOURGEOIS (collective) – VII, VIII, IX; DICHTERLIEBE (Heinrich Heine) – VIII; DOCTOR

FAUSTUS (Thomas Mann) – V; FANTASIA K475 (Mozart) – IV, VIII, IX; FAUST (Goethe) – VII; FORCE OF CIRCUMSTANCE (Simone de Beauvoir) – XI; FOURTEENTH SONATA, QUASI UNA FANTASIA (Beethoven) – X; GRETCHEN AM SPINNRADE (Goethe) – VI; IF (Rudyard Kipling) – I, II; JOURNAL (André Gide) – II; JOURNAL DE GUERRE (Ernst Jünger) – V; JUST SO STORIES (Rudyard Kipling) – I, XI; LA CROIX DE BOIS (Paul Harel) – II; LA ROSE ET LA RÉSÉDA (Aragon) – XI; LES ÉTUDES ET LA GUERRE (Stéphane Israël) – X; LES NOMBRES REMARQUABLES (François Le Lionnais & Jean Brette) – VII, IX; ON THE NATURAL HISTORY OF DESTRUCTION (W. G. Sebald) – VII, IX; PAINTING AT DORA (François Le Lionnais) – VII; PARIS DANS LA COLLABORATION (Cécile Desprairies) – V, XI; PÈRE GORIOT (Honoré de Balzac) – XI; POEMS (St. Thérèse of Lisieux) – II; ROBERT LE DIABLE (Meyerbeer) – III; SHOULD WE PARDON THEM? (Vladimir Jankélévitch) – XI; SURVIVAL IN AUSCHWITZ (Primo Levi) – VIII; THE CHARTERHOUSE OF PARMA (Stendhal) – VIII, IX, XI; THE DAMNATION OF FAUST (Hector Berlioz) – II; THE DIVINE COMEDY (Dante) – VII, VIII; THE DROWNED AND THE SAVED (Primo Levi) – IX; THE LIGHTS GO DOWN (Erika Mann) – VI; THE LOST ONES (Samuel Beckett) – VII; THE MASTER AND MARGARITA (Mikhail Bulgakov) – III, VI; THE NIGHT WATCHMAN OF PONT-AU-CHANGE (Robert Desnos) – VIII, XI; THE ODYSSEY (Homer) – VII; THE TWO GRENADIERS (Heinrich Heine) – I, V; THE TWO GRENADIERS (Heinrich Heine & Robert Schumann) – XI; TROILUS AND CRESSIDA (Shakespeare) – II; UN DÉPORTÉ BRISE SON SILENCE (Robert Francès) – VII, VIII, IX; UNE HISTOIRE MODÈLE (Raymond Queneau) – VII.

Thank you to all the authors of all these works, but also to Sébastien Balibar, Anne F. Garréta, Pierre Lévy, Sylvie Roelly, Olivier Salon, Norbert Schappacher, and Simone Weiller. Thanks to their help, this book could be written. It was composed mainly in Strasbourg and Paris, from October 2009 to September 2013.

Various places are mentioned (in alphabetical order): Africa, Aix-la-Chapelle, Alexandria, Alsace, Ardennes, Athens, Atlantic (ocean), Auschwitz, Bangor, Belgium, Berlin, Boston, Brittany, Buchenwald, Cambridge, Canaries (islands), Chartres, Chatou, Chemin des Dames, Clermont-Ferrand (Place de Jaude), Cologne, Digne, Dora, Douaumont, Drancy, Dresden, Europe, France, Fribourg, Germany, Hamburg, Holland, Istanbul, Italy, Kursk, Le Chesnay, Lodi, London, Lyon, Marseilles, Mediterranean (sea), Metz, Mexico, Midwest (American), Milan, Monowitz, Montluçon, Morocco, Moscow, Munich, N. (Goethestrasse, Humboldtstrasse, Marienfriedhof, Marktplatz, Schillerstrasse, the university), Nevers, Normandy, Oxford, Padua, Paris (Arc de Triomphe du Carrousel, Arc de Triomphe de l'Étoile, Rue d'Artois, Rue du Bac, Rue Blanche, Rue Caulaincourt, Avenue des Champs-Élysées, Pont au Change, Lycée Chaptal, Rue de Chateaudun, Rue de la Chaussée-d'Antin, Rue Claude-Bernard, Boulevard de Clichy, Place du Colonel-Rol-Tanguy, Avenue de la Croix, Rue Danielle-Casanova, Rue Dante, Rue Delambre, Square d'Estienne-d'Orves, Avenue Dubuisson, Place de l'Étoile, Avenue Foch, Avenue du Général-Lemonnier, Boulevard Haussmann, Avenue Hector-Berlioz, Invalides, Avenue d'Italie, Rue Lagrange, Lycée Louis-le-Grand, the arches of the Louvre, Hotel Lutetia, Jardin du Luxembourg, Gare de Lyon,

Hotel Majestic, Rue de Médicis, Rue de Ménilmontant, Rue Meyerbeer, Montmartre Cemetery, Montparnasse Cemetery, Gare Montparnasse, Rue Notre-Dame-des-Champs, Avenue de l'Opéra, Palais-Royal, Père-Lachaise Cemetery, Rue Pierre-Curie, Avenue Principale, Rue des Pyramides, Avenue Rachel, Hotel Raphael, Boulevard Raspail, Rue du Rohan, Pont Royal, Rue Saint-Dominique, Saint-Germain-des-Prés, Rue Saint-Jacques, Boulevard Saint-Michel, Saint-Philippe-du-Roule, Place Saint-Sulpice, Place de la Sorbonne, Rue Soufflot, Les Tourelles camp, Trocadéro, Jardin des Tuileries, Impasse de Valmy, Carrefour Vavin, Rue Véron, Rue du Vieux-Colombier), Petrograd, Poelkapelle, Poland, Russia, Saint-Maurice, Saint-Nazaire, Senegal, Sigmaringen, Spain, Strasbourg (Palais Universitaire, Vauban Stadium), Switzerland, Troy, United States, Upper Silesia, Vallorbe, Verdun, Vichy, Vienna, Warsaw, Weimar, Wölfersheim, Ypres.

INDEX OF PROPER NAMES

Guynemer (Georges): 32, 121

H   H. (Monsieur): 32-33, 35, 42

H. (Madame): 31-33, 35, 42, 122

Heine (Heinrich): 8, 70, 101, 103-104, 119, 122-123, 140, 145, 155

Hermann (Bernhardt): 61, 140–141

Hermann (Charlotte): 61, 75, 83-84, 134-135, 137, 141

Hermann (Wilhelm): 91, 134-136, 141

Hitler (Adolf): 47, 53-54, 71, 105

Homer: 94

Humboldt (Alexander von): 82

J   Jankélévitch (Vladimir): 153

Janvier (Albert): 16, 20, 24-25, 27, 30, 73

Janvier (Alphonse): 29

Janvier (Madeleine): 14, 16-18, 21, 24-25, 28, 30, 73

Janvier (Marguerite), *see* M. (Marguerite)

Janvier (Thérèse): 17-18, 25, 28-29, 34

Jaurès (Jean): 40, 43

Jesus: 24, 28

Jünger (Ernst): 62, 65, 77

K   Kant (Immanuel): 82

Karajan (Herbert von): 74

Kerensky (Alexander): 33

Kipling (Rudyard): 20

Klein (Louis): 112-113, 121, 130, 144, 154

Köchel (Ludwig von): 122

Kristoff (Kirill): 85

Kürz (Charlotte), *see* Hermann (Charlotte)

Kürz (Frau): 61, 84, 135, 137

Kürz (Heinrich): 55-59, 61-64, 66, 69-70, 74, 76, 79, 83-84, 86, 90-91, 93, 120-121, 125, 134-137, 141, 144, 146, 148-149, 152-153

L   Lagrange (Joseph-Louis): 67

La Martinière (Father de): 15, 29

Langlois (Guy): 72, 142

Langlois (Jean): 142

Langlois (Luc): 142

Langlois (Marc): 142

Langlois (Mathieu): 72, 128, 142

Langlois (Paul): 142

Langlois (Pierre): 142

Langlois (Thérèse): 34, 39, 72, 74, 128, 142

Leclerc de Hauteclocque (Philippe): 97

Legendre (Adrien-Marie): 86

Le Lionnais (François): 75, 94

Lenin (Vladimir Ilyich): 33

Liszt (Ferenc): 94

Lotte, *see* Kürz (Charlotte)

Lubin (Germaine): 74

M   M. (Anne), *see* Dubois (Anne)

M. (Antoine): 142

M. (Bernadette), *see* Meyer (Bernadette)

M. (Christian): 5-11, 18-30, 39, 45-46, 51, 55-56, 63-75, 77-78, 85-86, 89-93, 106-107, 119-121, 123, 125-129, 138, 141-144, 147-148, 150, 153-155

TRANSLATOR'S NOTE

This text—what is it, exactly? A literary experiment? A pile of documents? A history lesson? A research project? A reading list? A language game? A series of *exercises de style*? Or no more than an assortment of words and numbers?

Nothing like translation can lead you to so deeply question the nature of a literary text, especially when you're translating an Oulipian text. Although I didn't have to worry about avoiding certain letters or adhering to a fixed number of characters in each chapter,[1] the main difficulty of translating *One Hundred Twenty-One Days* was that, at times, it felt like eleven disparate translation projects. And one huge research project. My job, like that of the historian, was to look for connections between these disparate elements and make some sense out of them—my own.

In particular, the novel's structure, which combines eleven different stylistic forms and links their beginnings and endings with the same few words, proved far more challenging (but no less fascinating) than I first imagined. With each chapter came a new style and voice that had to both stand alone and fit into the text's whole. Like little Christian, I was asking all kinds of questions. What kind of diction would a World War I nurse use in her diary?

---

1   Examples of Oulipian constraints, respectively from Georges Perec's *La Disparition* (*A Void*, trans. Gilbert Adair) and Paul Fournel's *La Liseuse* (*Dear Reader*, trans. David Bellos).

How much should a transcribed interview sound like the way someone (and a very old someone at that) would speak? Just how many fragmentary sentences are permissible in a historian's notes for them to still be readable (despite all the warnings from my spell checker)? Can a series of locational cues take you on a walk through Paris even if you've never been there?

To find answers to some of these questions, I read into the text, as well as beyond it. After all, translators (like writers) are readers, too. So as I worked on this translation, I read lots of material: wartime newspapers, mathematics articles, psychological evaluations, historical diaries, transcribed interviews, and many of the books mentioned in the supernumerary chapter.

Beyond these questions of style, *One Hundred Twenty-One Days* is packed with references to literary works and real people, places, and events. In order to understand how all these references fit into the text, I researched them, in depth. First, I set out to read as many of the books listed in the supernumerary chapter as possible (then, judging this perhaps a bit too ambitious, narrowed my list down to those works that play more significant roles in the text, if not their most relevant parts). I also made a playlist of the songs referenced in said chapter, and listened to it often (usually while translating).[2] I even compiled over a hundred images on Pinterest depicting many of the people, places, things, and events (or their partial inspirations[3]) that appear in the novel, from a kapok tree

---

2   What if books came with their very own soundtracks?

3   You might like to know that some of the fictional characters and places in the novel are inspired by real people or places, often with several real figures converging into one fictional one.

in Senegal to various photographs of mathematicians[4] to all those historical plaques in Paris. Then, to get a better idea of where those plaques can be found, I took a virtual walk across Paris via Google Earth. And like any good researcher, I created a multi-tabbed Excel file to keep track of all kinds of information related to the text, including a timeline of the book's events, a list of the Library of Congress call numbers for the books in the supernumerary chapter, and a chart copied from Wikipedia with details on all the English translations of Dante's *Inferno* published before 1939.[5] You haven't seen any of this, but trust me, it's there in the translation. For me, at least.

★

Here's where I should probably say something about the differences created in the translation (which some might call "losses," but "differences" is a bit less negative, don't you think?). As Oulipian readers may have guessed, there are a few hidden constraints tucked into certain points of this book, such as the alphabetical list in chapter X and the parenthetical vocalic restrictions in chapter VII.[6] Without going into terrible detail (no one wants to read a long translator's note), let it suffice to say that I had to radically transform these passages in English in order to maintain the constraints.

---

4   There's even a photograph of two mathematicians sitting outside and petting a dog that smacks of the one mentioned in chapter VI.

5   Wikipedia: "English translations of Dante's Divine Comedy."

6   I made sure to ask Michèle for her permission to mention these constraints, since revealing constraints is a point of contention within the Oulipo.

For me, such transformations were the most thrilling part of the entire project.

Some of the other differences gained in my translation came about through the book's rich intertextuality—all those quotations from and allusions to other literary works. As a general rule for the quotations from foreign-language texts, I chose to use published translations where possible. While this is the usual practice for quoting works in translation, it also celebrates the work of previous translators and their contributions to the ever-changing intertextual network that is World Literature.[7]

 A familiar face cropped up in all this intertextuality in the references to two texts by Rudyard Kipling: his short story, "The Elephant's Child," and his poem, "If." Readers can decide for themselves how much or how little chapter I parodies Kipling's story—for me, it was a matter of inserting certain words and phrases from the story into my translation, which certainly created a different effect compared to if I had simply translated the chapter without looking at Kipling's text.

I also adopted a few strategies in other parts of the text to manipulate its heteroglossic nature, following what I saw as the text's own logic. For example, I rendered Harold Smith's letter in chapter X in British English, which seemed necessary given his Oxonian origin. I also followed the text's logic in chapter V when I wanted to add a footnote to explain an acronym; while footnotes are usually discouraged in literary translation, in this case my footnote blends right in with the 46 other footnotes in the chapter.

---

7   You will find a list of these translators in the Supernumerary Note, which follows this note.

As for the German words and phrases scattered throughout the novel, I chose to leave those alone, since translations have already been provided in the text itself.[8]

★

Before you close this book, please allow me to thank Michèle Audin, for her humility and openness to collaborate with me throughout this journey; David Dollenmayer, for his generosity in assisting my understanding of the Brecht quotations; my mentors Emmanuelle Ertel and Alyson Waters, for their infectious devotion to the art of literary translation; my parents, for their everlasting encouragement[9]; and my husband and best friend Jonathan, for his steadfast love and patience, not least in listening to my muddled attempts to express my translation struggles at the end of a long day's work, reading through my entire manuscript when I was sick of editing it, and coming up with a solution for one of the trickiest parts of this text.[10]

Christiana Hills
Binghamton, NY

---

8   In other words, no annoying translator's footnotes required.

9   And because you should honor your parents if you want to live a long life (Ex 20:12).

10   No telling which one, but a choice few of you already know.

SUPERNUMERARY NOTE OF SUPER TRANSLATORS

I would also like to thank the following translators for their exceptional work which, in various ways, found a place in this translation:

ALAN BANCROFT (*Poems of St Thérèse of Lisieux*, St. Thérèse of Lisieux), ANN HOBART ("Should We Pardon Them?", Vladimir Jankélévitch), ANTHEA BELL (*On the Natural History of Destruction*, W. G. Sebald), ARRAND PARSONS & LOLA RAND (*The Damnation of Faust* (libretto), Hector Berlioz & Almire Gandonière), C. K. SCOTT MONCRIEFF (*The Charterhouse of Parma*, Stendhal), CAROLYN FORCHÉ ("The Night Watchman of Pont-au-Change," Robert Desnos), DANIEL LEVIN BECKER (*Painting at Dora*, Francois Le Lionnais), DAVID DOLLENMAYER (*Conversations in Exile* (uncredited), Bertolt Brecht), DAVID LUKE (*Faust*, Johann Wolfgang von Goethe), GEORGE MUSGRAVE (*Inferno*, Dante Alighieri), HENRY WADSWORTH LONGFELLOW (*Inferno*, Dante Alighieri), KEITH WALDROP ("The Swan," Charles Baudelaire), RAYMOND ROSENTHAL (*The Drowned and the Saved*, Primo Levi), RICHARD HOWARD (*Force of Circumstance*, Simone de Beauvoir), SAMUEL BECKETT (*The Lost Ones*, Samuel Beckett), STUART WOOLF (*If This Is A Man*, Primo Levi).

Thank you all
for your support.
We do this for you,
and could not do
it without you.

DEEP
VELLUM

DEAR READERS,

Deep Vellum Publishing is a 501c3 nonprofit literary arts organization founded in 2013 with the threefold mission to publish international literature in English translation; to foster the art and craft of translation; and to build a more vibrant book culture in Dallas and beyond. We seek out literary works of lasting cultural value that both build bridges with foreign cultures and expand our understanding of what literature is and what meaningful impact literature can have in our lives.

Operating as a nonprofit means that we rely on the generosity of tax-deductible donations from individual donors, cultural organizations, government institutions, and foundations to provide a of our operational budget in addition to book sales. Deep Vellum offers multiple donor levels, including the LIGA DE ORO and the LIGA DEL SIGLO. The generosity of donors at every level allows us to pursue an ambitious growth strategy to connect readers with the best works of literature and increase our understanding of the world. Donors at various levels receive customized benefits for their donations, including books and Deep Vellum merchandise, invitations to special events, and named recognition in each book and on our website.

We also rely on subscriptions from readers like you to provide an invaluable ongoing investment in Deep Vellum that demonstrates a commitment to our editorial vision and mission. Subscribers are the bedrock of our support as we grow the readership for these amazing works of literature from every corner of the world. The more subscribers we have, the more we can demonstrate to potential donors and bookstores alike the diverse support we receive and how we use it to grow our mission in ever-new, ever-innovative ways.

From our offices and event space in the historic cultural district of Deep Ellum in central Dallas, we organize and host literary programming such as author readings, translator workshops, creative writing classes, spoken word performances, and interdisciplinary arts events for writers, translators, and artists from across the world. Our goal is to enrich and connect the world through the power of the written and spoken word, and we have been recognized for our efforts by being named one of the "Five Small Presses Changing the Face of the Industry" by Flavorwire and honored as Dallas's Best Publisher by *D Magazine*.

If you would like to get involved with Deep Vellum as a donor, subscriber, or volunteer, please contact us at deepvellum.org. We would love to hear from you.

Thank you all. Enjoy reading.

Will Evans
Founder & Publisher
Deep Vellum Publishing

LIGA DE ORO ($5,000+)

Anonymous (2)

LIGA DEL SIGLO ($1,000+)

Allred Capital Management

Ben & Sharon Fountain

Judy Pollock

Life in Deep Ellum

Loretta Siciliano

Lori Feathers

Mary Ann Thompson-Frenk
    & Joshua Frenk

Matthew Rittmayer

Meriwether Evans

Pixel and Texel

Nick Storch

Social Venture Partners Dallas

Stephen Bullock

DONORS

Adam Rekerdres

Alan Shockley

Amrit Dhir

Anonymous

Andrew Yorke

Anthony Messenger

Bob Appel

Bob & Katherine Penn

Brandon Childress

Brandon Kennedy

Caroline Casey

Charles Dee Mitchell

Charley Mitcherson

Cheryl Thompson

Christie Tull

Daniel J. Hale

Ed Nawotka

Rev. Elizabeth
    & Neil Moseley

Ester & Matt Harrison

Grace Kenney

Greg McConeghy

Jeff Waxman

JJ Italiano

Justin Childress

Kay Cattarulla

Kelly Falconer

Linda Nell Evans

Lissa Dunlay

Marian Schwartz
    & Reid Minot

Mark Haber

Mary Cline

Maynard Thomson

Michael Reklis

Mike Kaminsky

Mokhtar Ramadan

Nikki & Dennis Gibson

Olga Kislova

Patrick Kukucka

Richard Meyer

Steve Bullock

Suejean Kim

Susan Carp

Susan Ernst

Theater Jones

Tim Perttula

Tony Thomson

SUBSCRIBERS

Adrian Mitchell

Aimee Kramer

Alan Shockley

Albert Alexander

Aldo Sanchez

Amber Appel

Amrit Dhir

Andrea Passwater

Anonymous

Antonia Lloyd-Jones

Ashley Coursey Bull

Barbara Graettinger

Ben Fountain

Ben Nichols

Bill Fisher

Bob Appel

Bradford Pearson

Carol Cheshire

Caroline West

Charles Dee Mitchell

Cheryl Thompson

Chris Fischbach

Chris Sweet

Clair Tzeng

Cody Ross

Colin Winnette

Colleen Dunkel

Cory Howard

Courtney Marie

Courtney Sheedy

David Christensen

David Griffin

David Weinberger

Ed Tallent

Elizabeth Caplice

Erin Kubatzky

Frank Merlino

Greg McConeghy

Horatiu Matei

Ines ter Horst

James Tierney

Jay Geller

Jeanie Mortensen

Jeanne Milazzo

Jennifer Marquart

Jeremy Hughes

Jill Kelly

Joe Milazzo

Joel Garza

John Schmerein

John Winkelman

Jonathan Hope

Joshua Edwin

Julia Rigsby

Julie Janicke Muhsmann

Justin Childress

Kaleigh Emerson

Ken Bruce

Kenneth McClain

Kimberly Alexander

Lea Courington

Lara Smith

Lissa Dunlay

Lori Feathers

Lucy Moffatt

Lytton Smith

Marcia Lynx Qualey

Margaret Terwey

Mies de Vries

Mark Shockley

Martha Gifford

Mary Costello

Matt Bull

Maynard Thomson

Meaghan Corwin

Michael Elliott

Michael Holtmann

Mike Kaminsky

Naomi Firestone-Teeter

Neal Chuang

Nhan Ho

Nick Oxford

Nikki Gibson

Owen Rowe

Patrick Brown

Peter McCambridge

Rainer Schulte

Rebecca Ramos

Richard Thurston

Scot Roberts

Shelby Vincent

Steven Kornajcik

Steven Norton

Susan Ernst

Tara Cheesman-Olmsted

Theater Jones

Tim Kindseth

Todd Jailer

Todd Mostrog

Tom Bowden

Walter Paulson

Will Pepple